Sweet Potato Kisses: A Friendsgiving Romance

Published by Legacy Literary House

North Carolina, USA

Cover design by Legacy Literary House

ISBN (paperback): 979-8-218-87469-8

www.legacyliteraryhouse.com

Printed in the United States of America

First Edition : Month 2025

Sweet Potato Kisses

A Friendsgiving Romance

Nina Stewart

Table of Contents

Author's Note

Welcome to Sweet Potato Kisses. Thank you so much for picking up this cozy little holiday romance. This book is Hallmark-movie inspired, for the romance girlies who love slow-burn moments, soft chemistry, friendship, found family, and the beauty of Black love on the page. If you're looking for steamy or spicy scenes, this isn't that book. My hope is that Brandy and Sullivan make you smile, breathe a little easier, and remember that love can be gentle, safe, and unexpectedly sweet.

Thank you for reading. It means more than you know.

With Love,

Nina

Chapter 1

Brandy Williams stared at the can of pumpkin pie mix like it had personally ruined her life. It sat there...shiny, smug, perched in her palm as if it didn't know she'd spent the last fifteen minutes pacing up and down the baking aisle at Pine Hill Market trying to decide whether to bake pumpkin pie, sweet potato pie, or lie about baking.

The store smelled like cinnamon broomsticks and cloves. Autumn light poured through the front windows, catching the rows of pumpkins stacked near the door. Out on Main Street, yellow and orange leaves swirled around like it was a movie set.

Inside, Brandy's mood was anything but picturesque.

This was supposed to be the year. The perfect Friendsgiving. The year she'd walk into Ryan's house wearing matching fall outfits with Dante, hand in hand, smiling like they were already someone's holiday greeting card. Instead, she was debating pie filling in the middle of the store, alone, with half a grocery list and a whole broken engagement weighing her down.

She flipped the can in her hand, sighed, and muttered under her breath.

"Pumpkin or sweet potato... somebody pick for me."

The woman in the next aisle gave her a quick side-eye and kept walking. Brandy closed her eyes for a second, trying to center herself. She still had to pick up caramel, apples, and puff pastry before she stopped by Maplewood Nursing Home to help Ms. Lee bake turnovers for the residents. Because apparently heartbreak didn't cancel community service. And Friendsgiving was in a week.

Her cart squeaked forward as she tossed the pumpkin can in with a loud clang, the sweet potatoes she grabbed earlier finally had some

3

company in the lonely cart. That's when she heard it, low, warm, and teasing.

"Brandy? Are you arguing with pumpkin pie filling?"

Her stomach dipped, not in panic, but in anticipation like the slow climb before a rollercoaster tipped over the top. She turned, and there he was. Sullivan Harper. Tall. Handsome. Gray hoodie, layered under a camel-colored coat, dark jeans, and brown Timberland boots, looking like he'd stepped straight out of the "XXL Magazine" cover. Fresh fade, skin dark like mahogany and a picture-perfect smile. He was still fine as hell. He smelled good too. Only this was real life, and Sullivan was standing in her grocery store holding a bag of Gala apples and that crooked grin she'd always hated liking.

"Sullivan!?" she blurted, eyebrows shooting up.

"What are you doing here? Don't you usually spend Thanksgiving somewhere with a skyline and room service?"

She didn't even hesitate; she wrapped him up in a hug. Not a polite, church-lady pat either. A real one that lingered on a bit longer than expected.

"Came home for a bit," he said, rocking back on his heels like he hadn't just thrown her whole afternoon off-balance. Voice deep and smooth like silk.

"Ryan's been texting me about Friendsgiving for weeks. Figured it was time." She folded her arms over her chest, lips tugging into something that wasn't quite a smile.

"Is that Sullivan Harper?" a young woman whispered to her friend.

Brandy noticed the way Sullivan pretended not to hear; suddenly extremely interested in adjusting the apples in his hands, but she caught the flicker of embarrassment in his eyes.

"Wow. A real-life celebrity in Pine Hill. Should I alert the press?"

"Don't start," he laughed. "I'm just a man trying to buy apples."

They stood there for a moment, letting the weight of their shared history fill the space between them. The last time she'd seen Sullivan, it was at Homecoming three years ago. He'd been busy, charming, untouchable. She'd been... still holding on to a dream with Dante.

"Sooo," he said, nodding toward her cart. "What's the great pie debate?"

She rolled her eyes.

"Pumpkin or sweet potato? And don't say pumpkin. You're not allowed to be wrong."

"Sweet potato, obviously. What kind of question is that?"

She laughed for the first time all day.

"Thank you. Somebody with sense. Because I was losing my mind."

"Always had it," His voice dropped just enough that something in her chest tightened. She looked away first.

"Well... good luck with the apples, big shot." She nudged her cart forward, trying to remember why she came here in the first place.

"Bran...wait."

She paused. He hadn't called her by that nickname in years.

"You going to Friendsgiving?" he asked.

She hesitated. "I don't know. I'm still debating. I was supposed to bring Dante but I'm sure Ryan and her big mouth already told you we broke up" she blurted, not even familiar with her own voice and its betrayal.

He chuckled.

"Uhhh nope. She hadn't mentioned any of that. But that's good to know."

He leaned forward on his shopping cart, eyes catching hers. For a moment, she forgot how to breathe. The way he looked at her, steady, curious, a little too familiar. That made her suddenly aware of everything about herself.

The loose curls brushing her cheek. The faint sheen on her lip gloss. The burnt orange turtleneck sweater and jeans she'd thrown on, now feeling too casual.

She caught her reflection in the freezer door beside them, deep brown skin, curls soft and haloed by the fluorescent light, that same smile she hadn't seen in weeks.

And she realized she'd missed feeling like this.

Like herself.

"Hey, since you're not bringing a plus one, we can pop up there together. I'm not bringing anyone either."

His voice glided over her like warm honey.

"You should come. I want to catch up with the crew and it wouldn't be the same without you."

He grabbed her hand like it was the most natural thing in the world, fingers warm against hers. For a second, she forgot how to breathe. She couldn't tell whether he was flirting or just being his charismatic self but either way, her heart didn't get the memo."

"Uhhh yea. I'll think about it. Hit me up later. I'm running late to the nursing home."

By the time she reached the register, Brandy had talked herself into going to Friendsgiving. Breakup or not, she wasn't about to hide at home like her whole life had fallen apart. She could show up, bring her pie, smile a little, and at least pretend she wasn't still bruised on the inside. And if she happened to run into Sullivan again...well, that wasn't the reason she was going. She was going for her friends. Not him. At least, that's what she kept telling herself, even as her pulse said otherwise.

Chapter 2

The kitchen at Maplewood Nursing Home smelled like caramel, cinnamon, and a little bit of peace. Brandy had always loved that smell. It reminded her of everything simple and good. But today, even the sweetness sat heavy against the ache in her chest. She stood at the counter, spreading apple filling over thin sheets of puff pastry, her hands moving on autopilot. It was easier to keep them busy than to think too hard.

"You're quieter than usual, baby," Ms. Lee said from across the room. She was plating turnovers like she'd been running a bakery her whole life, headwrap tied neatly, gold hoops glinting in the warm kitchen light.

"You okay?"

Brandy let out a short breath.

"Yeah... just thinking."

"Mhm." Ms. Lee's tone was a knowing hum. She didn't push. She never did.

The truth tingled under Brandy's skin like static. One hour ago, she'd been sulking over pumpkin pie mix, trying to convince herself she didn't care about Friendsgiving. Now Sullivan Harper had shown up out of nowhere; smelling woodsy and sweet, looking like a walking reminder of how soft her heart used to be. And worse, how it still wanted to be soft. She pressed the pastry edges a little too hard.

"I bumped into an old friend."

That earned her a sharp look over the rim of Ms. Lee's glasses.

"Mmm. Do tell, young lady."

Brandy tried to smile.

"His name's Sullivan Harper. We went to college together; back when life was simpler and I still thought crushes were supposed to hurt.

Ms. Lee chuckled, sliding a tray into the oven.

"So that explains the faraway look on your face."

Brandy's laugh came out soft and uneven.

"It's not like that. Okay, maybe it used to be like that. But he's different now. Big-shot author, whole career, always traveling. I just..."

Her voice trailed off, the truth catching in her throat. She wasn't supposed to feel this way. Not now. Not when Dante's words still echoed in her mind: *I'm just not ready.* Not when she still blamed herself for loving someone who never showed up the same way. Ms. Lee caught her silence, turned, and read her face.

"This about that fiancé of yours?"

Brandy nodded, eyes glistening.

"Ex-fiancé." She swallowed hard.

"Three years of being engaged, three years of waiting for him to be ready. Then one day, he tells me I'm not ready. Like I haven't been planning forever. Like I didn't already picture the house, the holidays, the life."

Her throat burned. The words came out in pieces now.

"And I stayed, Ms. Lee. I kept hoping he'd change, that maybe love could convince him. But love shouldn't have to beg."

Ms. Lee crossed the room, wiped her hands on her apron, and took Brandy's trembling hands in hers.

"Oh, baby girl... sometimes the people we build our futures with are only meant to be part of the blueprint, not the house."

Brandy's lip quivered. "Then why does it still feel like I messed it all up?"

"Because you loved him with your whole heart."

"And when love doesn't go the way we planned, it's easy to think it's our fault. But sometimes God's not saying no...He's saying, not that one. Sometimes He's got something better waiting, but He needs to tear down the plan you made so you can walk into the blessing you didn't see coming."

Brandy blinked back tears, staring at their joined hands. Ms. Lee's words didn't erase the pain, but they settled somewhere deep, like truth finding a home in her chest. She thought of Sullivan then. Of the way his voice had wrapped around her name like a promise. Maybe Ms. Lee was right.

And for the first time since the breakup, she wasn't just grieving what she'd lost, she was terrified of what she might feel again. Ms. Lee gave her hand one last squeeze before standing.

"Now dry those eyes before you season the turnovers with tears," she said with a wink, moving back toward the oven.

"And don't go burnin' my pastries thinking about that man."

Brandy let out a shaky laugh, wiping her cheeks.

"Yes, ma'am." The timer dinged, the smell of sugar and spice curling through the air. Ms. Lee pulled out the tray, golden and perfect, setting it between them.

"See?" Ms. Lee said, sliding one toward her.

"Sometimes, baby, what rises after the heat is the sweetest part."

Brandy's eyes softened as a quiet smile formed, breaking the warm pastry in half. The steam lifted between them sweet, soft, healing. The ache in her chest eased just enough to let in a little light.

Chapter 3

Sullivan Harper wasn't supposed to be back in Pine Hill. He was supposed to be in New York, holed up in some overpriced hotel suite with bad room service, cranking out edits his publisher was breathing down his neck for. But there he was, standing in the baking aisle of Pine Hill Market with a bag of Gala apples, looking like a man who'd made three wrong turns and accidentally stumbled into his past.

He still didn't know what made him get in the car and drive down from the city. Maybe it was the way the cold had started to feel different this year. Maybe it was the ache of silence that came when the book tour ended. Or maybe... it was the way Ryan had texted him in all caps:

Ryan: *DON'T EVEN THINK ABOUT GHOSTING FRIENDSGIVING THIS YEAR.*

Ryan: *We've been nice for 3 years. This is your year, sir.*

He chuckled, shoving his free hand into his coat pocket. He hadn't seen the crew since that last homecoming trip three years ago. The idea of walking into Ryan's house again after so long made something small and nervous crawl into his chest.

He didn't go straight home after the grocery store. He sat in his car for a minute, keys still in the ignition, the heater humming against the November cold. The bag of apples rested in the passenger seat, like some kind of evidence that today didn't go how he planned. He exhaled slowly, letting his head fall back against the seat.

He saw her today.

Brandy.

She hadn't changed. Well...she had. But not in the ways that mattered. That wholesome, grounded energy she carried was still there. She'd always been the softest corner of their friend group. And seeing her standing there in that aisle, glasses tilted on the brim of her nose, debating pumpkin pie filling like the world depended on it, made him forget whatever speech he'd rehearsed about why he "didn't have time" to come home. His phone buzzed in the cupholder.

Jackson.

He answered with a quiet laugh already sitting in his throat.

"Man, you finally answered," Jackson said, laughter in his voice.

"I was two seconds away from calling Ryan to send a search party." Sullivan smirked "Yeah, yeah. I've been busy."

"Busy hiding," Jackson shot back.

"We ain't seen your bougie ass in years. You know Ryan's already planning some dramatic entrance for you. We were about to cast you off the island."

He laughed, shaking his head. "She doesn't change."

"Not even a little," Jackson said.

"But for real, Van, it's good you're coming. We missed you, man."

There was a beat that made Sullivan realize he'd missed them too.

"Yeah," he said softly. "Yeah, I missed y'all too, bro."

"You coming solo, right?" Jackson asked, voice casual but curious.

"Of course!" Sullivan answered a little too fast. "You know me."

"I can ask Gabby to bring one of her single homegirls. You know, give you a nice Lil yeah on the side." Jackson broke out laughing at his own joke.

Sullivan rolled his eyes, but a laugh slipped out anyway. "Nah, bro, I'm good. Last time you tried to hook me up, I almost had to get a restraining order."

"Aight, aight!" Jackson wheezed. "She wasn't that bad. Wasn't she your inspiration for one of your books? That joint made you a bestseller. We even!"

Sullivan shook his head, still laughing. "Yeah, thanks for that trauma."

"Still married to the hustle, huh?"

"Something like that," Sullivan murmured.

He didn't have to explain. Jackson knew. Everyone did. He'd spent the last few years chasing deadlines, tours, interviews, podcasts, the whole bestselling author cycle. And when you're always moving, it's easy not to notice how quiet your life gets.

"Just so you know," Jackson added, "Ryan's got this whole Friendsgiving extra this year. Lights. Matching mugs. Probably gonna have a camera crew. You know she's an 'influencer' now. So, bring your holiday spirit."

"I'll try not to ruin the aesthetic," Sullivan didn't bother hiding his sarcasm.

"Good man." Jackson's voice softened. "And hey... it's okay to actually enjoy it this time. Unplug a little."

When the call ended, Sullivan sat there a moment longer, phone still warm in his hand. He scrolled to Ryan's name and hit call before he could talk himself out of it. She answered on the first ring.

"Look who decided to remember we exist!"

He laughed. "I'm in town."

"WHAT! Wait. HOLD ON, HOLD ON. You're in town? Like, actually here? Not on a connecting flight to somewhere cooler?"

"Yep. Grocery store and everything."

"Oh my God," she squealed. "This Friendsgiving is about to be legendary. Do you hear me? Legendary. I need a picture of you standing in front of the Welcome to Pine Hill sign because this feels like a fever dream.

Sullivan grinned despite himself. "You're still dramatic, sis."

"And you still love it," Ryan shot back. "I'm so happy you're here. Where are you staying? Debbie's?"

Debbie was his mom. And no, he was not posting up there. His mother meant well, but one look at him on her doorstep and she'd start fussing over him. She'd start in on her *"you're not getting any younger"* speech and somehow end with a conversation about grandbabies. He didn't need that kind of pressure today.

"Now you know damn well I'm not staying at my mom's," he said, a small smile tugging at his mouth.

"She'll have plenty of time to drive me crazy after she gets back." He leaned back in the seat, still replaying the way Brandy smelled like vanilla and baked cookies.

"She's on her cruise. She will be home tomorrow. I figured I'd surprise her."

Ryan's voice jumped back in, full of curiosity and just a pinch of attitude. "Ohhh, okay. So, where you holed up, knucklehead?"

"Dang, Ry, you stay in my business," he said, laughing. "But if you must know, I'm at an Airbnb over on Clover Street."

"I mean, you could stay here with us. Save ya coins." Ryan and her husband had this huge house. It was way too big for just the two of them, but she'd always said it was for the future babies.

"I did consider it," Sullivan admitted. "But I need some time alone. My agent begged me to relax. And we both know if I stay at your house, I'll end up tangled in garland by day two."

"Oh boy, bye!" Ryan laughed. "Ain't nobody about to have you decorating nothing." She paused, then softened.

"Well, the offer stands. I gotta hop off...I have a podcast to record; but I want to see you at the house Saturday. I'm helping Brandy with some food baskets for the community, and we need to see you before Friendsgiving."

The sound of her name was like a small spark under his ribs. "Yeah. I, uh... saw her."

"Saw who? Brandy?!" Ryan's voice shot up an octave. "You already saw her? How? Where?"

"Grocery store."

Ryan gasped like this was breaking news. "Sullivan Harper, this is God's plan."

"Ryan."

"No, no, this is a rom-com opening. I can feel it in my spirit."

"Hear me out," she continued. "Brandy and Dante just broke up. I know you're not into anything serious. Both of you need some...companionship. Are you catching what I'm putting down right?"

Sullivan rubbed his hand down his face but couldn't stop the laugh from breaking through. "I'm hanging up now."

"You better think about it," Ryan sing-songed before the line clicked.

He ended the call, shaking his head as he rested his hand on the steering wheel, letting the heater blow warm air across his knuckles. The book tours were loud. Interviews even louder. Cities all blur together when you're always passing through them. People knew his name, his books, his face-but not him. Not really.

Home wasn't just a place. It was the people who remembered him before the world did.

And he'd been away too long. He merged into the slow familiar beat of Pine Hill traffic.

The streetlights cast a soft amber glow over Main Street. Pine Hill hadn't changed much; maybe a new coffee shop, maybe a new bench, but it still smelled like home. And for the first time in a long time, the idea of being surrounded by people who knew him didn't feel like a distraction.

It felt like something he'd been needing.

Chapter 4

The cinnamon candle was fighting for its life. Ryan leaned across the kitchen island, her short jet-black bob falling just above the collar of her oversized burgundy sweater. The buttons pulled slightly as she stretched, flashing the pale orange tank top underneath. Petite but never quiet, she had a way of taking up space without ever needing to be tall.

She struck the lighter again and whispered, "You better not embarrass me in front of company," like the wax could hear her. The flame finally caught, flickering warm against the soft orange glow of the string lights she'd hung along the cabinets.

"Mmhm." She stepped back, hands on her hips. "Now that's cozy."

Holiday jazz floated through the house from her playlist, while the oven hummed low in the background. Every surface looked like a Pinterest board had exploded: folded plaid napkins, miniature pumpkins, eucalyptus stems she didn't need, and a white ceramic platter that read *Grateful* like a classy social media caption.

Ryan wasn't famous-famous, but she'd built a life she loved.

After college, while everyone else was scrambling into nine-to-fives, she'd leaned into what she did best, making things pretty and making people laugh.

Five hundred thousand followers and thirty brand deals later, she was the unofficial "aesthetic queen" of Pine Hill.

Not a celebrity. Just Ryan. The friend who would fix your living room, your outfit, and your attitude in one afternoon.

Her phone buzzed on the counter. FaceTime.

She swiped up. "Hey boo," Desiree sang through the screen.

"Hey hun! What's up?" Ryan grinned.

"Girlllll...how many candles do you own?" Desiree squinted at the warm glow behind her.

"Mind your business," Ryan shot back.

Desiree cackled. "I bet it smells like Bath & Body Works had a baby with an apple pie."

Ryan snorted, flipped her camera, and panned across the kitchen: lights, garland, and the shiny copper mugs she'd scored on clearance.

Fabian had just shaken his head earlier when she started opening all her Amazon and FedEx boxes of garland and decorations. "Can we get through Thanksgiving first?" he'd said. And yet, every year, he still ended up untangling lights beside her.

Desiree snapped her fingers. "This is vibes, babe. I love it."

Ryan adjusted the phone with freshly manicured fingers, the soft glint of her nails catching the soft kitchen light. "Aye! You know I do my thang when it comes to decorating," she said with a playful wink.

"Decorating? Girl, this is a full renovation," Desiree laughed, her phone propped on a tripod as she blended her eyeshadow.

Desiree had been doing makeup since her psych-major days in college, long before she dropped out junior year to chase it full-time. Now she owned her own "The Glam Spot" the only beauty bar in Pine Hill, booked solid every day, and has beat the face of more than one small-time celebrity.

For a moment, Ryan just stood there-bare feet pressed into the cool hardwood, one hand resting on the island. It wasn't quiet. It was homey.

And it hit her.

She missed them. Not just the parties or the cider or the one pan of rolls she always burned. She missed them. The crew. All of them crammed into one room, talking loud, talking over each other, laughing until somebody choked.

Brandy used to sit on the counter, sipping some fruity flavored wine cooler and pretending not to like the chaos. Sullivan used to lean against the wall, too cool for everything, but smiling the whole time.

Desiree and Jackson? The life of the party. Desiree brought the music and liquor; Jackson dealt cards and started Spades, Uno, or Dominoes like it was a championship.

That ache in her chest loosened, replaced with a stubborn spark. This Friendsgiving wasn't going to be just another gathering. This year was going to feel like old times.

"Ry? Are you even listening?" Desiree snapped her back to reality.

"Yeah, girl," Ryan said, moving toward the mantel.

"Mhm," Desiree muttered, going on about her new boo thang.

Ryan flicked on the garland lights. The living room bathed in a golden glow. Perfect.

"Oh wait, Dez," Ryan cut in. "Did I tell you Sullivan's back?"

Desiree froze mid eyeshadow swipe. "Oh really?"

Ryan's grin spread slow. "Uh huh. And guess who he bumped into at the grocery store?"

Desiree's lips curled. "Oh no."

"Oh yes." Ryan smirked.

"Brandy?" Desiree fully committed now.

"Yep."

Desiree snorted. "Awwww, that's cute. Van's probably a whole weirdo now. You know how those celebrity types act."

Ryan stayed quiet.

Desiree caught it. "Brandy is not even feeling him like that anymore. She's probably still sniffin' behind lame-ass Dante," she said, lining her lips with nude liner.

More silence.

"Ryan. No ma'am. Don't even think about it."

Ryan tossed a burnt orange throw over the couch, all fake innocence. "What? God's plan is God's plan."

Desiree groaned. "Don't start."

"I'm not starting anything," Ryan lied. "I'm just... setting the scene."

Desiree rolled her eyes. "Well... Brandy could use something to get her mind off Dante. He's still a clown for that mess."

"Yeah," Ryan sighed softly. "I just want our girl to be happy."

"And you think Van can do that for her?" Desiree's tone dripped with skepticism.

"Well," Ryan said with a little smirk, "They're both going through a season. Maybe they can support each other."

Desiree laughed. "Support? Yeah, okay."

LATER THAT NIGHT, RYAN sat cross-legged on the couch with her iPad balanced on her knees, half watching a holiday baking show, half scrolling through Sullivan's latest tour posts. All those glossy photos, fancy hotels, bookstore lines, interviews with Gayle King and Tamron Hall. It looked glamorous.

But she'd known him too long. She saw the spaces between the smiles. The quiet in his eyes. Sullivan Harper had been moving so fast, he'd forgotten what stillness felt like.

She opened her messages.

Ryan: *Don't flake on me Saturday. I'll drag you out of that Airbnb myself.*

Sullivan: *Wouldn't dream of it.*

Ryan: *Wear something flannel. I'm building a vibe.*

Sullivan: *Of course you are.*

She smirked. Same Sullivan. Rolling his eyes through the phone, probably.

Her fingers hovered over Brandy's name. Brandy had been quieter than usual lately, and quiet never fooled Ryan. She'd seen her friend love hard, break harder, and tuck those bruises neatly behind a soft smile.

She started typing.

Ryan: *Hey girl. We still good for Saturday? I grabbed some cute baskets for the families.*

Brandy: *Yep! All good. I'm excited and can't wait to see what ideas you've come up with.*

Ryan: {Brown Heart Emoji}

Short reply. Too short. But it was something.

Ryan locked the screen, leaned back, and let the smooth jazz settle into the room. The wind brushed the window, her cinnamon candle doing its best to make the house feel warmer than it was.

This Friendsgiving was going to hit differently. She felt it in her bones.

Not perfect just... different.

She closed her eyes. "Alright, Lord. I'm trusting you on this one."

A smile tugged at her lips. She lifted her cider in a quiet toast.

"Let love do what it does."

Chapter 5

Brandy pulled up to Ryan's house and had to laugh. Of course it looked like a fall Pinterest board come to life. The two-story brick home glowed against the late afternoon light like it knew it was the star of a holiday movie.

A dozen plump pumpkins lined the front porch steps; each one perfectly arranged like they'd auditioned for the spot. Twinkle lights wrapped around the white porch banister, climbing all the way to the roof like golden vines. A rustic wooden sign by the door read *Grateful. Thankful. Blessed.* in swoopy cursive, because Ryan never did anything halfway.

It smelled faintly of cinnamon and roasted apples even from the car. Brandy popped the door open, clutching the strap of her crossbody bag. She wasn't nervous. She and Ryan had done this holiday basket project every year since college, it was their thing. The comforting rhythm of pulling out baskets, sorting food, tying ribbons, and delivering smiles to families in need.

What she was anxious about was Ryan looking at her with that face. The one that asked how she was really doing without saying the words. The one that saw through every "I'm fine" she'd ever tried to sell.

The irony wasn't lost on her. Family therapist, queen of holding space for other people's emotions... and she couldn't even talk about her own.

As she climbed the porch steps, Sullivan Harper's grin flickered through her mind like an uninvited commercial break. Easy. Smooth. Unexpected. She shook her head sharply.

"Not today, heart."

The front door was unlocked, because Ryan treated her friends like family and Brandy pushed it open. The buttery scent of apple cider wrapped around her like a hug.

Ryan was in full host mode. Apron tied snug at her waist, bob bouncing as she moved around the kitchen like she was auditioning for a Food Network holiday special. Cinnamon sticks floated in a steaming pot on the stove. A mellow jazz playlist played softly through the house. She was finishing up a livestream on her phone, voice bright and animated.

Brandy leaned against the doorframe, smirking.

"Lord, I just know you got something good planned for us to eat."

Ryan turned with a grin, hitting the "end live" button like a pro. "And that's why I keep you around because you know I don't play when it comes to Friendsgiving."

"You don't play about a lot of things," Brandy said, toeing off her boots. "Like seasonal décor."

Ryan gave a dramatic hair flip and pointed to the pumpkin display behind her. "Exhibit A."

They moved easily into their usual rhythm. Ryan talking, Brandy listening with just enough side commentary to keep things rolling. Ryan filled her in on Fabian's long shifts at the hospital. Brandy updated her on clients at the practice, how she was maybe considering pivoting or expanding her services in the new year.

Ryan opened a pantry door and started pulling out cans and boxes, stuffing, cornbread mix, jars of apple butter. Brandy grabbed the baskets from the closet by the entryway. The table quickly filled with ingredients waiting to be sorted.

Ryan brushed her hands on her apron, glanced up at her friend, and softened.

"So..."

Brandy froze for half a second. She knew that tone.

"Ryan," she warned.

"How are you really?" Ryan asked quietly.

The question landed like a weight between them.

Brandy took a slow breath, fiddling with a bag of cranberries. "I haven't heard from him," she said finally, voice lower than before. "I expected he'd at least call or... something."

Ryan leaned a hip against the counter. "You think maybe he's got somebody else?"

Brandy's mouth twisted. "I don't know. I don't even want to think about it."

But she already had.

Last night, against her better judgment, she'd checked Dante's Instagram. There he was, posted up with his boys in the Poconos, all smiles and whiskey glasses. A *"guy's trip."* He'd never taken one before. Her mind had been spinning ever since, trying to decide what hurt more: his silence or how easily he looked like he'd moved on.

Ryan reached over and gave her wrist a quick squeeze. "You don't have to talk about it if you don't want to."

"Good," Brandy muttered, exhaling slowly. "Because I really don't."

They both turned back to the baskets, slipping into the familiar comfort of movement and purpose. Sorting, organizing, bagging. No heavy words needed.

Then the doorbell rang.

Ryan glanced at the oven timer, the smell of pumpkin tarts warming the kitchen.

"Brandy, can you get the door? I don't want my tarts to burn."

Brandy wiped her hands on a dish towel and walked toward the door, the kitchen light spilling softly into the entryway.

The late fall air slipped in as she pulled it open, and then there he was.

Sullivan Harper.

He wasn't bundled up like some stranger passing through. No. He looked like he belonged on a holiday card. A burnt orange flannel hugged his broad shoulders, the sleeves pushed up just enough to show strong forearms. A chocolate-brown T-shirt peeked out beneath, and the dark wash jeans he wore fit like they'd been made to sit on narrow hips and long legs. A brown Carhartt beanie sat low on his head, a little crooked, like he'd tugged it on in a rush.

And maybe it was the chill in the air, or maybe it was him but her breath caught anyway. He tilted his head, lips curving into that easy grin that used to get him out of trouble back in college.

"Didn't expect you to be the welcoming committee."

She didn't say anything right away. Couldn't. Her eyes flicked from the flannel to the grin to the way his breath fogged in the cold, like he'd just stepped out of a Hallmark movie scene she didn't sign up for.

Sullivan shifted his weight, raising a brow as he lifted the canvas tote bag in his hand, a mix of canned goods and pie mix peeking out the top.

"So... are you going to let me in?" he said, drawing out the words just enough to make it playful. "Because it's freezing out here."

That snapped her out of it.

Brandy blinked hard, straightened her spine, and crossed her arms like she hadn't just been caught staring.

"Right. Sorry. Just.... wasn't expecting company."

"Ryan invited me," he said easily, like the two of them standing there wasn't doing strange things to her pulse.

She stepped aside, the corners of her mouth threatening a smile she refused to let fully form. "Of course she did."

As he stepped past her, the faint scent of cedarwood, warm spice, and cold air followed him in. And just like that, her stomach did that annoying flip again.

Brandy followed Sullivan into the kitchen, tossing the dish towel over her shoulder to keep her hands busy. He moved with an easy confidence that came from knowing this house, this crew, this season.

Ryan looked up from the counter where she was tying a bundle of cinnamon sticks with twine, her grin wide and entirely too pleased with herself.

"Right on time!" she sing-songed, like she hadn't just set her best friend up.

"Hey, Ry," Sullivan said, lifting the bag in a casual salute.

"Look at you following the dress code," she teased. "You understood the flannel assignment."

Sullivan chuckled. "What can I say? I'm a good guest."

Brandy shot Ryan a narrow look, one that said oh, I see what you did, but Ryan pressed her lips together and lifted her brows, the corners of her mouth twitching like she was holding back a laugh. The picture of I-did-nothing-but-actually-I-did.

Sullivan set the bag on the counter and started unloading cans. Apple pie filling. Cranberry sauce. Cornbread mix. He pushed his sleeves a little higher, the soft flannel bunching at his elbows. The muscles in his forearms shifted as he started lining up the cans, neat and steady, like this was just another ordinary chore. Brandy's fingers stalled mid-ribbon tie. She tried to focus on the basket in front of her but her gaze snagged on him anyway.

She cleared her throat, grabbing a bag of sweet potatoes just to do something with her hands.

"You always pack baskets like you're doing inventory?" she asked, her tone light, teasing.

Sullivan looked up, a grin tugging at the corner of his mouth. "What can I say? I'm a man of order."

"Order?" She arched a brow. "You just lined up four cans like they're auditioning for a cookbook cover."

He glanced at the lineup, laughed under his breath. "Aye, don't do me like that. I like some order every once in a while. Plus, I'm a writer. We make everything dramatic." He laughed.

Brandy shook her head, but her lips curved despite herself. "Good to know some things don't change."

"And what's that?" he asked, leaning casually against the island.

"You still find a way to be extra, even with canned goods."

Their laugh filled the kitchen, smooth and low, threading right through the music and the scent of cinnamon. And when he looked at her again, really looked, it felt like the air got just a little thicker between them.

Ryan watching her plan unfold decided to slip out of the kitchen with a breeze, "I'm gonna grab more baskets from the garage. Y'all keep going without me."

The way she said y'all made Brandy want to throw a cinnamon stick at her. That left Brandy and Sullivan standing side by side at the kitchen island. The house stirred around them, jazz low, cider simmering, string lights winking across the cabinets.

Sullivan glanced at the pile of food like he was about to confess something. He held up a roll of ribbon like it might bite him.

"So... full disclosure," he said, his grin crooked and boyish, "I have absolutely no idea what I'm supposed to be doing."

Brandy pushed her glasses up the bridge of her nose, curls falling softly around her face as she tried, unsuccessfully to keep the laugh out of her voice. She shifted her weight to one hip, the oversized cream sweater draping effortlessly over her curves, and gave him a look that was equal parts amused and unimpressed.

"You mean Mr. Bestselling Author doesn't know how to pack a basket?" she teased, her eyes narrowing just enough to make it playful.

Sullivan lifted his hands in mock surrender. "I can build a world, but apparently not a holiday care package."

She shook her head, a tender smile tugging at her lips, and handed him a can like she was giving him a second chance at life. "Then it's a good thing you've got me."

"I write about people who know what they're doing," he said, rubbing the back of his neck. "I'm still trying to catch up."

She huffed out a soft laugh. "Here."

She slid a basket toward him and showed him how to layer the heavier items first, tucking paper lining around the edges. He tried to mirror her movements. He almost did. Then the basket tilted and a can of yams rolled out and clanged to the floor.

She bit her lip, hard, trying not to laugh. "Off to a great start."

He crouched to grab the fallen bow, his shoulder brushing her hip as he stood. The touch was nothing, barely there at all, but it still sent a warm flicker through her.

"Sabotage," he said with mock seriousness. "You're trying to make me look bad."

She shook her head, smiling before she could stop herself. "You don't need my help for that."

Their eyes caught for a beat just long enough for something soft and familiar to spark between them. Not heavy. Not forced. Just a quiet little pull she felt in the center of her chest.

"So, you do remember how to be around regular people," she teased.

He tilted his head, lips curving in that way that always used to undo her. "I never forgot. I just... forgot how much I missed it."

That tugged at something deep. She dropped her gaze, pretending to focus on the basket as she tucked a box of stuffing inside.

For a few minutes, they moved in an easy rhythm-stacking, arranging, nudging elbows. She made fun of his tragic folding skills; he pointed out how seriously she took basket aesthetics. Their laughter wounds through the cinnamon-warm air, settling between them like an old inside joke.

Then their hands reached for the ribbon at the same time. Her fingers grazed his steady, warm, familiar enough to make her breath catch. Neither of them pulled away. The room didn't go silent, but it felt like it narrowed to that single point of contact.

His thumb brushed her knuckle, an accident... or close enough to feel like one. Her pulse stuttered anyway.

She hadn't been this close to him in years.

Close enough to breathe in that warm cedar spice of his cologne.

Close enough to see the way his flannel pulled across his shoulders when he leaned in, the clean line of his jaw when the corner of his mouth flicked up.

In college, she'd liked him.

But now... now her attention kept snagging on little things she didn't let herself notice back then. Her pulse gave her away long before her mind caught up. This wasn't supposed to feel like anything. It was just a basket. A ribbon. A friend.

Not a rom-com moment where the air shifted and the world felt too small for two people pretending nothing was happening.

Brandy cleared her throat, willing her heartbeat to calm down.

Not today, heart. We're not doing this.

Sullivan didn't say anything, but she caught the flicker of a smile at the corner of his mouth like he noticed the shift in the air too. He didn't push. He just stayed there beside her, steady and quiet, like he belonged.

And then Ryan's voice called from the hall, "I heard laughter. Y'all better not be eating the snacks without me."

Brandy snatched her hand back like she'd been caught stealing. "We're just working."

Sullivan smirked. "Yeah. Working."

Ryan walked back in with more baskets, clocking their faces in one sweeping glance and raising a brow. She didn't say anything. She didn't have to. Brandy focused hard on straightening a basket that didn't need straightening. But her heart was still doing that annoying little flip.

And Sullivan? He was still grinning like he knew exactly what he'd done.

BY THE TIME BRANDY got home, she slipped into the quiet of her living room, still carrying the warm scent of cinnamon and cedar on her sweater. She sank onto the couch, phone in hand, her heartbeat not quite settled from the way Sullivan's fingers had brushed hers earlier.

A vibration buzzed against her palm.

Sullivan: *Tonight was... nice. Unexpected, but nice.*

Brandy's lips curved before she could stop them. She typed slowly.

Brandy: *Yeah... it was. Really nice.*

A few seconds passed, then another bubble appeared.

Sullivan: *I'm glad I got to see you before Friendsgiving.*

(pause)

You are going, right?

The question nudged at her chest curious, careful, but wanting the truth.

Brandy hesitated, thumb hovering before she finally typed:

Brandy: *Yea... I'm going. You know I wouldn't miss it.*

(pause)

I was and kinda still am in my feelings about a few things. But I'm not letting that stop me from enjoying friends and family.

The dots popped up instantly.

Sullivan: *Good. You deserve a night that feels like joy again.*

Her breath caught soft, sweet, unexpected.

Another bubble appeared before she could recover.

Sullivan: *And for what it's worth... I'm really looking forward to seeing you there.*

Heat crept up Brandy's neck. She bit her lip, cheeks warming in a way she hadn't felt in a long time.

She didn't text back.

She didn't need to.

That last message settled warm and deep in her chest like the beginning of something she wasn't ready to name but couldn't ignore anymore.

Chapter 6

The group chat was chaos.

Ryan: *Everybody clear your calendars for Tuesday evening. Pine Hill Corn Maze. Y'all down?*

Desiree: *Girl, what is this? A kindergarten field trip? And on a Tuesday?!*
Ryan: *Fall vibes, heaux.*
Sullivan: *Y'all don't got jobs? Nah, seriously....a Tuesday is wild.*

Jackson: *Bro, I know you not talking! You can write anywhere, fam lmfao. But real talk, Ry... on a Tuesday?*

Gabby: *I'm bringing the Hennessy! *wink*
Ryan: *my favorite person.*

Ryan: *Nah, y'all lazy. It's just a couple of hours. We get there at 6 p.m. and stay for a few. I just want to see y'all.*

Desiree: *Girl, you will see us at Friendsgiving rotf*
Brandy: *Lord.*
Sullivan: *What is Fabian saying about this last-minute trip?*
Desiree: *Right. But Fabian be in on her mess too!*
Jackson: *Facts! lmao*
Ryan: *See, now y'all not about to do me! Y'all better have your behinds there!*
Desiree: *Dang girl. Ok. But you not about to keep bullying us to be "festive."*

Brandy laughed out loud as she scrolled through the thread, her mug of chamomile steaming beside her. The chat never changed, loud, messy, and familiar in the best way. Even Sullivan was chiming in more than usual, which was rare. He'd gone quiet for years.

She typed back.

Brandy: *I'll be there.*

It was short. Safe.

She didn't even try to lie to herself about why she felt that small flutter when Sullivan reacted with a single pumpkin emoji.

THE PINE HILL HARVEST Patch looked like it had been designed by a Hallmark movie set decorator. Pumpkins lined the entrance in perfect little rows, twinkle lights wrapped around every fence post, and the scent of hot cider and cinnamon hung in the air like a hug. A breeze swept across the open field, rustling the cornstalks and making the string lights flicker softly.

Brandy climbed out of her car and tugged her soft knit sweater tighter against the bite in the air. The November sun still held a trace of warmth, but the breeze carried a chill that hinted at winter's edge.

Ryan and Fabian were, of course, the first to arrive. Fabian's arm was draped around her shoulders, her burnt-orange knit beanie tilted just so, their smiles bright enough to sell cider in bulk. Ryan already had her phone out, narrating their entrance for her Instagram Stories.

Brandy shook her head, laughing as she approached. "Y'all really came dressed for your Hallmark debut, huh?"

Ryan twirled, striking a mock pose. "You already know. I was born for this aesthetic."

Fabian grinned, shaking his head. "She's been talking about this all week."

Before Brandy could respond, another voice called out.

"Look who's here," Jackson said, smile wide and easy. He towered over most of the crowd, lean and relaxed, the russet tone of his skin catching the late-afternoon sun. His low taper fade was fresh, and for once, the man wasn't in a suit. Instead, he wore a black fleece zipped to his neck, a matching beanie, and black khakis.

Pine Hill's favorite lawyer actually looked... relaxed.

No briefcase. No courthouse scowl. No earbud stuck in his ear like he was ready to cross-examine somebody in the parking lot.

"Wow, look at you not dressed like you're about to defend someone's freedom," Brandy teased.

Jackson rolled his eyes. "Aye, but I clean up nice though, right?" He struck a pose like he was auditioning for GQ.

"Boy, you are crazy!" Brandy laughed.

At his side, Gabby looked like autumn personified. Her long honey-colored locs were tucked beneath a cranberry duffle coat, and the soft scent of patchouli with a whisper of sage floated around her as she hugged Brandy. Her energy was grounded and mellow, lingering like incense smoke.

"Girl," Gabby said with a soft grin, "You look like you needed this."

She gave Brandy that knowing look...the *girl, I know men can be a mess look. It was* a look without judgment but understanding.

Brandy chuckled. "You have no idea."

Desiree showed up next, arm hooked around her new boo, Marcus, the tall, fine, and entirely clueless one. His cream Henley was rolled at the sleeves like the chill in the air didn't apply to him.

Desiree, meanwhile, looked every bit the Chicago girl she was, rocking acid-washed cargo jeans, a red crop top, a Bulls bomber jacket, and a fresh pair of J's. Soft life era activated.

And then Sullivan appeared.

Brown fleece. Matching Carhartt beanie. Jeans and a pair of Timberlands that crunched against the gravel path. One hand tucked in his pocket, the other wrapped around a steaming cup of cider.

Brandy felt her heartbeat trip over itself.

"Hey, Bran," he said, voice low and smooth, carrying that easy, lazy charm that hadn't faded over the years.

"Hey yourself," she managed, willing her voice to sound steady.

Desiree, a step behind her, raised her brows so high Brandy could practically hear the teasing without a single word.

"Y'all ready to get lost in some corn?" Jackson clapped his hands, the unofficial hype man as always.

Once everyone grabbed cocoa and snapped their mandatory group photo (courtesy of Ryan's influencer heart), they entered the maze.

It didn't take long for Desiree to start in.

"So," she said, bumping Brandy's shoulder, "How's your heart handling the whole breakup with Dante?"

Brandy sighed. "Dez, I'm not trying to think about him right now."

"Well, he's a damn clown for what he did."

Desiree tilted her head toward Sullivan, who was walking up ahead with Jackson. "Mhm. So what's up with you and Van? Y'all had a little meet-cute moment earlier?"

Brandy grabbed her friend's arm, pulling her closer in a playful tug as they rounded a bend. "There is absolutely nothing going on with us. I don't even know what you're talking about."

Marcus trailed behind them like lost luggage. He was handsome, broad-shouldered, skin rich like polished cocoa, but clearly clueless about what was going on.

"Babe, where's the exit?" he asked.

Desiree sighed dramatically. "I don't know, Marcus. Follow the corn."

Brandy snorted.

"Don't laugh at me," Desiree shot back, though she was laughing too. "Anyway, love... I know you don't want to think about wack-ass Dante, but you know what they say....the best way to get over someone is to get under someone else."

She laughed so loud that Jackson and Sullivan turned around like she'd set off a firecracker.

"Shhh!" Brandy giggled, heat rising in her cheeks.

"No, seriously," Desiree continued, eyes bright with mischief. "It's been, what, over a month now?"

"Yeah," Brandy admitted quietly. "Four weeks is too soon to be thinking about any of that."

Desiree raised a brow, already unlocking her phone. "Girl, please. Four weeks too damn long. And look." She shoved the screen in Brandy's face.

There he was, Dante. Smiling near a fireplace, arm draped over another woman's shoulders.

"Damn, Desiree! You just couldn't let me be?" Brandy snapped, stepping back. "I don't want to think about this right now."

"Oh, so it's my fault?" Desiree shot back, lifting her chin. "I'm trying to help you stop moping over a man who strung you along for three boring years!"

Brandy's temper flared. "Ohhh, yep. Tell me exactly how you feel. Why do you even care? It's not your damn life. And at least I can get a man to propose. You're out here with a new meathead every week."

The air between them cracked like dry corn husks.

Jackson and Gabby moved between the two before it could go further. Marcus looked around like someone had dropped him in the middle of a soap opera.

"Aye, now y'all need to chill," Jackson said, holding up his hands.

"Nah," Desiree muttered, gripping Marcus's arm, "let her stay lost. I'm just telling her to stop wasting her time sniffing after Dante."

Desiree opened her mouth again, probably to say something guaranteed to make Brandy's skin crawl, so Brandy turned on her heels and walked down another path.

"Bran!" Desiree called after her.

Sullivan glanced back. One look at Desiree's smug little grin told him everything he needed to know.

"Nice work, Dez," he muttered, jogging after Brandy. "Bran, wait up."

The sound of crunching leaves faded as they moved deeper into the maze. Rows of golden stalks framed the narrow path, the air crisp and sweet with the scent of kettle corn drifting from the festival grounds.

Sullivan caught up easily, falling into step beside her.

"Yo, wait up," he said, a little breathless but light. "What was that all about?"

She blew out a slow breath, fogging the chill in the air. "Nothing. Desiree just knows how to piss me off."

For a few beats, they just walked. The wind rustled through the stalks, their boots crunching softly against the dirt path. The quiet wasn't awkward. It wrapped around them like the fall air, a little fragile, and oddly safe.

"You ever build your whole future around someone," Brandy said finally, her voice a low, steady ache, "and then they just... hand it back like it was nothing?"

Sullivan slowed his steps, letting her set the pace. He didn't rush to fill the silence.

"I waited for Dante," she whispered. "First for the relationship. Then for the proposal. Next for the date. Three years of planning a life together. And then one night, he sends me a message and said he wasn't ready."

Her laugh came out soft, sharp around the edges. "Said I wasn't ready either. Like I hadn't been holding the pieces for him while he made up his damn mind."

The wind stirred the cornstalks, their dry rustle filling the quiet. Sullivan felt it sit heavy in his chest, not just her words, but how she carried them, tucked deep beneath all that calm.

"I don't know Dante like the others do," he said quietly, "but I do know that wasn't fair to you."

She didn't look at him, but something in her shoulders eased.

"Yeah," she breathed.

They reached a fork in the maze, the sun dipping low and painting everything in gold. Sullivan hesitated for a second, then shrugged out of his jacket and draped it gently over her shoulders.

"Can't have you freezing out here."

Her heart stumbled over itself at the warmth still clinging to the fabric.

She didn't say thank you. She didn't need to. Their eyes met, just long enough for something quiet and unspoken to settle between them. The air shifted, softer. Closer. Sullivan held her gaze, and for the first time in a long while, he didn't feel like he was passing through. He felt like he was exactly where he wanted to be.

By the time they made it back to the group, everyone was gathered near the apple shooter booth. Ryan and Fabian looked like a fall catalog cover. Jackson and Gabby were laughing over mini cinnamon donuts. Desiree was pretending she still wasn't upset from their argument. Desiree could irritate her soul and defend her in the same breath.

That was just who she was, blunt, loud, and loyal enough to snatch a wig for Brandy if it came down to it.

One of the workers squinted, then nudged her coworker.

"Girl... that's Sullivan Harper."

"Who?!" her friend said, a little too loudly as she craned her neck for a better look.

"He wrote If This World Were Mine. You know, the book our club read last spring."

Her voice dropped into a breathless whisper as recognition hit. Now she was full-on starstruck, staring at Sullivan like he might disappear.

The whole group heard it, and Jackson was not about to let the moment slide.

"Yeah, that's him!" he hollered, grinning. "Y'all want an autograph? Sullivan loves the fans!"

He laughed so hard he nearly dropped his donut, while Sullivan shot him a look and motioned for him to chill.

Too late.

The damage was done.

The women hurried over with their phones out, snapping pictures like he was a whole celebrity sighting, which he was.

Brandy didn't even turn around. She kept walking toward the apple shooter like she was on a mission, determined not to get swept into the commotion.

She stepped closer to the booth, eyeing the bright red apples stacked in the basket. "Five dollars for three shots? Easy," she said, slipping a bill into the metal tin before anyone else could volunteer.

Ryan cackled. "Girl, be careful. I need you beautiful and not bruised for Friendsgiving."

"Ha ha. Don't worry about me. I got this. It looks easy enough." Brandy shot back, rolling her shoulders like she had something to prove. She stepped behind the cannon, squinting at the targets like they might rearrange themselves into something obvious. Gripping both handles, she clicked the red buttons that controlled the launch.

The cannon fired with a sharp whoosh, jolting her backward and nearly knocking her off her stance. A few people chuckled under their breath.

Brandy huffed. "It's fine. I got this."

She absolutely did not have it.

Sullivan stepped in behind her, close enough for his breath to stir a curl against her neck.

"You're holding it wrong," he murmured, voice low and smooth, a little closer than necessary.

Her pulse skipped. She could feel the heat of him on her back, steady and unhurried.

"Am I?" Brandy tilted her head, aiming for playful, but the rasp in her voice gave her away.

He chuckled. Warm and quiet before his hands brushed over hers, guiding them into place. His fingers lingered just a beat too long, not gripping, just there. Enough to make the rest of the world narrow to the space between them.

His palm skimmed her forearm as he adjusted her elbow. She felt the drag of his skin against hers, slow and careful, like a secret they hadn't decided to say out loud yet.

"Now," he whispered behind her ear, "shoot."

She drew in a breath and released the apple. It sliced through the air, hit the bell square, and rang out a crisp ding.

The group exploded into cheers. Ryan's scream rose above the noise, triumphant.

"I got that on video!" she shouted, waving her phone like she'd just secured an exclusive. "Y'all look so cute I might cry."

Brandy rolled her eyes, but her cheeks were flushed, her skin still tingling where his hand had been. Sullivan just laughed under his breath, like he'd felt it too.

A few feet away, Ryan's thumbs flew across the screen.

Fall in Pine Hill hits different #FriendsgivingSeason.

Miles away, Dante's scroll slowed.

And stopped.

Chapter 7

The drive home from the corn maze left a soft ache behind, like laughter you wished could last a little longer. She still smelled kettle corn on her sweater and felt the weight of Sullivan's jacket draped over her arm on the passenger seat.

She dropped her keys on the entryway table, kicked off her boots, and curled up on the couch with a blanket and her phone. Her thumb hovered over his name longer than she'd admit before she finally typed:

Brandy: *Hey*

Brandy: *Thanks for walking me through the maze earlier.*

His reply came faster than she expected.

Sullivan: *Anytime. You looked like you were about to disappear in there.*

She laughed softly.

Brandy: *I was two steps from hitchhiking out of that corn*

Sullivan: *Dramatic. But I respect it.*

The conversation slipped into something comfortable and familiar.

Brandy: *What time are you heading to Ryan's on Thursday?*

Sullivan: *Not sure yet. prob around 5ish.*

Brandy: Are you bringing wine or dessert?

Sullivan: *I was just gonna bring my charming personality.*

Brandy: So... nothing

Sullivan: Rude.

Sullivan: Fine. I'll grab something.

She stretched out, the glow of her phone lighting her smile. It wasn't forced.

It wasn't heavy. It just felt good.

Brandy: Bring a Riesling or a Tawny port. I've never known you to be

a good cook.

Sullivan: Oh ok. I see what you're doing. Don't do me like that. I can

make a mean mashed potato.

Brandy: Mashed potatoes? Puhlease lol.

Sullivan: Yes ma'am lol. butter, salt, little garlic. and my secret ingredient.

Brandy: Oh, do tell, sir.

She settled deeper into the blanket, feeling like a teenager on the phone past curfew.

Sullivan: Ok but if I hear you told anybody, it's me and you. on sight.

Brandy: Cross my heart.

Sullivan: I boil the potatoes in chicken stock.

She stared at the screen, then laughed out loud.

Brandy: THAT'S the secret? I thought everybody did that!

Sullivan: Oh hell no. There's folks out here making mashed potatoes with

straight sink water.

Brandy: Not sink water

Sullivan: Facts . Reminds me of our first Friendsgiving.

Brandy: The dorms? The janky turkey??

Sullivan: Yeah. and Ryan burned half the mac and cheese.

Brandy: and Jackson brought that store-bought pie like it was gourmet.

Sullivan: and you showed up with those yams. Best thing on the table.

Brandy: You remember that?

Sullivan: Yeah. I remember.

Something warm settled in her chest

Brandy: *Good times*
Sullivan: The best.
Sullivan: Sooooo what would you say if I picked you up for Friendsgiving?
Brandy: Oh wow, so we're still doing that?
Sullivan: Yeah. Why not? I meant what I said at the store.
Brandy: I know. I just didn't think too much about it. but yeah... I'm down.
Sullivan: Bet. Will I see you again before then?
Brandy: ....

Brandy looked at their thread, thumb pausing midair. Her shoulders softened, breath loosening. For the first time in weeks, the quiet didn't feel heavy. It felt comfortable. Like there was a possibility for something more.

She hadn't realized how loud life had been until now, tucked beneath a blanket, smiling at her phone like she was sixteen again. And then her phone buzzed.

Not from Sullivan.

Dante: *hey.*

Three letters. One tiny word.

Her smile faltered. The cozy warmth of the night shifted.

She didn't open it right away. She just sat there, the weight of three years and one unfinished future pressing against the quiet.

Chapter 8

ONE TINY MESSAGE.

Hey.

Her smile faded.

"Hey?" she whispered, her voice edged with disbelief. That was it? Weeks of silence, not a single call. Not a "how are you?" Not an explanation. Just... hey.

Her chest tightened. She thought about how he hadn't even faced her. How he'd sent his mother to pick up his things like she was just some box to be checked off. And then, as if that wasn't enough, his little boys' trip to the Poconos popped into her head.

Cute. Real cute.

She stared at the message so long the screen dimmed. Her fingers tightened around the phone until her knuckles ached. Like clockwork, she took a screenshot and dropped it into the group chat labeled "My Girls" just her, Ryan, and Desiree. The three of them had weathered everything together: college, bad men, and worse decisions. If anyone knew how to hold her up when her heart wobbled, it was them.

The replies came fast:

Desiree: *Oh I KNOW this clown did not message you "hey."*

Brandy: *Girl yes! I'm so pissed.*

Ryan: *See now I was trying to let him live but he needs to be checked.*

Desiree: Most definitely. What the hell does he think this is??

She let their indignation wash over her, but her pulse was still pounding.

Brandy: *and he knows what he's doing. hasn't said a word to me since*
he

called off the engagement.

Ryan: *Don't respond. He clearly wants attention.*

Desiree: *Oh, I know EXACTLY why he's messaging you.*

Brandy: *Why?*

Ryan: *Yeah, do tell friend.*

Desiree: *He's still lurking on social media!*

Brandy frowned, typing back:

Brandy: *Huh?*

Desiree: *Ryan posted all those cute ass corn maze and pumpkin patch*
pics.

And she tagged YOU and VAN.

Ryan: *Damn you right! I just checked and he's still following me. I'm*
about

to block his ass!

Brandy: *So, he got the nerve to be jealous but posted up in the Poconos*
with an IG model?

Desiree was relentless:

Desiree: *Nope. Don't block him yet. let him simmer. See he thought*
he was

just gonna keep Brandy as his little go-to thang. Didn't think Van
would show up this year. Didn't think he'd have competition.

Brandy's thumb hesitated over the keyboard.

Brandy: *Wait. wait. wait. There is nothing going on with me and*
Van.

We just cool. chillen.

Desiree: *Hmmm*

Ryan: *Ummmm friend, Van been feeling you. It just never been a*
good time. Now IS the perfect time.*

Brandy: *Time for what?*

Ryan: *Girl!! Time for you to be happy. To have a little romance.*

Desiree: *True, True. I mean Van's a square to me but he's waaayyy better than Dante.*

Brandy: *rolling eyes emoji

Ryan: *You know what, respond. give his ass a dry ass "what's up."*
don't give him the satisfaction of thinking you're waiting around for his call.

Desiree: *Yep. He's a clown.*

Desiree: *and if he responds.... which he will. You tell him y'all are done!*

Brandy set her phone on her lap and stared at the ceiling for a long moment. Her heart was tangled. Part of her wanted answers. Another part just wanted quiet.

She typed a reply, deleted it, typed again.

"What's up?" the words stared back at her. Flat. Too small for everything she wanted to say. But maybe small was all she had in her tonight.

Her thumb hovered, then she pressed send.

The screen lit up almost instantly, but not with the reply she expected.

Dante's name flashed across her phone. He was calling.

Still saved as Hubby.

Her breath caught. She hadn't changed it.

"Of course," she whispered, sliding her finger across the screen.

"Hello," she said softly.

The house, once so easy to be in, suddenly felt a little too quiet.

Brandy's stomach dipped, not in the soft, fluttery way Sullivan's name did, but sharp, like a stone skipping too fast across water.

"Hey, babe." His voice hit her the same way it used to. Low and a little rough. That familiar ruggedness that used to undo her when they were good.

"Don't babe me," she echoed, an attitude seeping through her tone. She hated how he made her feel.

"Aww, Brandy, baby don't be like that." Humor in his voice

"You sound tired." A soft chuckle followed, practiced and easy.

"Still overthinking like always?"

She pressed her lips together. Gaslight, page one of the Dante playbook.

"I'm fine," she said.

"What do you want, Dante?" she asked, the edge in her voice slipping out before she could stop it.

"I saw that little video Ryan posted. You at the corn maze with him."

The way he said *him* landed sharp.

"Yeah," Brandy said slowly. "Sullivan was there."

Another pause. A soft exhale that wasn't quite a laugh. "Guess that explains why I haven't heard from you."

Brandy's jaw tightened. "You haven't heard from me because you haven't called. For weeks."

"Babe, come on," he said, the old endearment sliding in like honey. "I just needed time. You know that."

"Time to do what?" she asked, voice firming. "Disappear?"

"Time to think. Everything got... heavy. We were fighting. I didn't wanna keep hurting you."

She closed her eyes. He was good at this. Twisting things just enough so that she felt guilty for his mistakes.

And then, in that same soft, practiced tone, he said, "I miss you."

That was the dagger. Simple. Familiar. Worn down to a blade.

"I'm cutting my trip short," Dante continued. "I'll be back tomorrow night. I wanna see you, baby. Just... talk. Fix this."

Her heart stuttered. For three years, all he ever had to do was say those words, and she'd fold. But tonight, she didn't feel small. Just tired.

"You called off our engagement," she said softly. "You don't get to pop back in because you saw a video."

"I didn't cancel us," he said quickly. "I just wasn't ready to rush something that's too important. You know me. I just needed space. But seeing you with him" he laughed like it was harmless, but it wasn't.

"I just realized I don't wanna lose what we have."

There it is, Brandy thought. Not love. Possession.

"You're not losing anything, Dante," she said. "Because you already let it go."

Silence hung in the air. She could hear his breathing, a little sharper now. The way it always got when she refused to budge.

"I'm coming back," he said again, lower this time. "We can talk after the holiday. I know you. You don't just give up."

That was the thing. She didn't give up. She held on too long.

"Dante...." she started, but he cut in.

"Just... think about it, babe," he said softly, the hook slipping in smooth. "We were supposed to get married. That doesn't just go away."

And for a moment, it worked. The words hit the bruise he'd left behind, and she felt it ache.

"Goodnight, Dante," she said, because anything else would pull her under.

"Goodnight, Brandy."

The line went dead.

Brandy set the phone down on the couch beside her, heart pounding and not with excitement, but with confusion. She curled into the blanket until it almost swallowed her whole.

She wanted to text Sullivan. She wanted to not want to text Dante. But instead, she did neither.

THE NEXT DAY BRANDY threw herself into her work like it might drown out the sound of Dante's voice.

Wednesday blurred by in a haze of tasks she didn't really need to do. The hum of the copy machine became white noise. The soft glow of her computer screen felt like a hiding place. At lunch, instead of eating, she drove straight to Maplewood Nursing Home and volunteered an extra hour.

She spoon-fed Miss Lila her vanilla pudding the way the woman liked it, slow and with patience. She pretended Mr. Walter's war stories weren't the same ones he always told. It was easier to listen than it was to think. Easier to care for someone else than sit with the ache knocking at the back of her chest.

Her phone buzzed once in her pocket. She stepped into the hallway. Ms. Lee watched her go, eyes deep and knowing.

Sullivan: *Hey*, been thinking about you. How's your day going?

The message hit low in her stomach, that soft flutter she'd tried to ignore last night.

Brandy: Hey it's... a day. I'm using my lunch to volunteer at Pine Hill Nursing Home.

Sullivan: *She serves the community too.* A beautiful woman with a *generous heart. I love it.*

Brandy huffed out a breath that was half-laugh, half-release.

Brandy: I try. Sometimes folks just need company.

Sullivan: How about I steal you for coffee? My treat. A little kindness for the caretaker.

She stared at the message a second longer than she needed to.

She could go back to work.

She could drown herself in productivity.

She could pretend last night didn't mean anything.

But she didn't want to.

Brandy: ...I could use a pick-me-up. Maple & Main? 10 mins?
Sullivan: *Bet. See you there.*

WHEN SHE PUT HER PHONE down, Ms. Lee was still watching her. That woman didn't miss a thing. She lifted her chin and mouthed, "Go." Then winked. Brandy couldn't help the stupid smile that tugged at her lips.

Chapter 9

Maple & Main smelled like cinnamon, pumpkin spice, and warm pastry dough. Holiday lights were already strung along the ceiling beams, and the playlist was pure soul-Christmas; Donny Hathaway and The Temptations humming in the background. She spotted him immediately.

Sullivan sat tucked into a small nook in the corner, jacket draped over the back of his chair. His shoulders were broad beneath his sweater, relaxed but strong, like he could carry weight without complaining about it. His eyes found hers, something in his expression shifted, gentle and easy.

Beside the counter, a small display shelf held a neat stack of his newest book, If This World Were Mine. Brandy stared at it for a moment.

Something unsure shifted inside her, a tiny voice reminding her that Sullivan lived in a world much bigger than Pine Hill.

She must've hesitated longer than she thought because Sullivan's expression changed. His eyes softened, brows drawing together just a little, like he could sense the wobble in her chest before she even formed the thought. Without a word, he stepped closer and pulled her chair out for her.

"You okay?" he asked quietly, not prying, just checking in.

Brandy blinked, forcing a small smile.

"Yeah. Just... thinking."

He seemed to understand more than she said.

As she moved to sit, he shifted in with her, the warmth of him brushing against the cold she hadn't noticed she was carrying. At the same time, a woman at a corner table lifted her phone like she was taking a picture of her muffin... though her camera was pointed directly at Brandy and Sullivan. He noticed almost instantly.

Without making it a big moment, Sullivan touched her elbow, gentle, steady, and grounding.

"Come on," he murmured, voice low enough for only her. "Sit. You're good."

He steadied her chair, then helped her slip out of her burgundy puffer coat. They sat. For a moment, neither spoke. The silence wasn't heavy, just full, warm, and careful.

Brandy looked up at him. He looked at her at the exact same time.

They both paused.

Then

"Hey," she said, breath catching a little too quickly.

"Hey," he echoed, but his came out softer, almost like he'd been waiting for her to say something first.

She smiled without meaning to.

He smiled because she smiled.

The moment stretched... sweet, awkward, and kind of perfect.

"I'm glad you came," he said, leaning back just a bit but keeping his eyes on hers.

"You really saved me," Brandy said, breaking the softness with a laugh. "Work is dragging, and clients are canceling sessions left and right. Though I already know they're gonna try to schedule last-minute after Thanksgiving once the family drama hits."

He grinned. "Oh, absolutely. Holiday season always brings out the confessions and the existential spirals."

"Right?" She laughed for real that time, and it loosened something inside her chest.

"I wanted to see you," Sullivan said. "Away from everybody else. It feels like we've always existed in groups. Never... just us."

Brandy looked down at her hands. "Yeah. It's always been Dez or Ryan. Or-"

"Dante," Sullivan finished, voice gentle but curious.

Before she could answer, a barista stepped up.

"Ma'am, you ready to order?"

Brandy exhaled, quiet relief. "Yes. Can I get the twelve-ounce pumpkin cinnamon latte with oat milk? And... the honey butter croissant."

Once the barista walked away, she rolled her eyes lightly.

"Yes. Dante."

Sullivan leaned back, not prying just listening.

"So... it's really over?"

"It is." She stared at the table, voice low but sure. "I think I've been in that relationship by myself for a long time. And admitting that out loud is...hard"

She swallowed. "I'm still figuring out what to do with that."

He nodded. His eyes softened.

"I get it. I spent years writing about love I wasn't really feeling. That kind of loneliness hits deeper than being alone does."

Brandy looked up surprised.

"You never settled down? But I never heard about you out here running through women either."

His mouth curved. "I had my moments."

But his tone said he'd always been careful with hearts including his own.

Their drinks arrived. Her croissant steamed.

"So," she said, tearing off a piece, "back in college... did you really-"

"Have a crush on you?" He didn't even blink. "Yeah."

Brandy froze. "Wait, what?"

"You were a freshman. I was trying not to be that guy." He shrugged like it was obvious. Like there was no world where he risked her feeling unsafe.

Her heart stuttered.

"I had the biggest crush on you too," she confessed, voice half-laugh.

His eyes lifted to hers, slow and direct.

"So... is the timing better now?"

Brandy playfully squinted at him. "Well... we are both single, right?"

Sullivan laughed. "Yes. Very single. Why you looking at me like I'm lying?"

"Just verifying." She grinned.

The conversation slid easy after that, teasing Ryan's over-achiever decorations, Jackson's meme addiction, and Dez being Dez. Brandy's laughter shifted from polite to real, open, and unguarded.

Time had a funny way of slipping when she was laughing. When the conversation felt easy. When she didn't have to guard her words.

Her phone lit up on the table. Lunch had ended fifteen minutes ago.

"Lord," she murmured, pushing her chair back. "Before I get fired..."

Sullivan stood when she did easy and natural. He reached for her coat before she could.

He held it open, and she eased into it, the movement steady and unhurried.

He was close now. Close enough for her to catch the warm spice and cedarwood on his skin. Close enough to notice how gentle his hands were, even in something as simple as helping her with a sleeve.

Her stomach did that small somersault again.

This time, she didn't pretend she didn't feel it.

"Friendsgiving tomorrow," she said, her voice coming out softer than she meant. "Wear forest green."

His mouth curved, slow. "Oh, so we matching?"

Brandy let the smile come. "Something like that."

They fell quiet. Brandy didn't feel the need to fill it. Neither did he.

Sullivan nodded once, he understood exactly what wasn't being said.

"Bet."

She walked out with her half drunken latte warming her hands and the cold air nipping at her cheeks. The world looked the same, but something in her felt... lighter. Not swept away. Not tumbling. Just... present.

She didn't name it and she didn't rush it. She didn't try to make it mean more than it did.

She just let herself feel it.

And for the first time in a long while, the feeling didn't scare her.

Chapter 10

The first thing Sullivan did every morning was whisper, "Thank you, God." The words slipped out before his feet even touched the floor. This was a quiet habit that had carried him through years of hotel rooms, long book tours, and lonely mornings in cities that didn't feel like home. But Pine Hill did. Or at least... it was starting to again.

The Airbnb gave a soft groan when Sullivan swung his legs out of bed, the floorboards creaking like an old friend clearing its throat. He padded across the cool wood in bare feet, the faint smell of cedarwood and last night's rain clinging to the room.

Cold water snapped him fully awake, mint burning fresh on his tongue. By the time he laced up his running shoes, the world outside had begun to stretch itself open, sky pale blue, sunlight threading through bare branches, breath rising like smoke.

The first few strides were stiff. Then his body found its rhythm, easy and familiar, like it always did. The quiet street rolled out in front of him, the maple trees shedding their last gold and orange leaves. One brushed his sleeve on the way down, landing at his feet. He didn't stop, just watched it spin once before the wind carried it off.

Somewhere between mile two and three, she slipped into his head.

The way her laugh had surprised him. The warmth of her hand against his.

He hadn't expected that. Not from Brandy. Not from this place.

His pace quickened. The cool air stung his cheeks, but it felt good, like breathing something honest. By the time he hit the bend near the old track, his chest had loosened, the noise in his head fading until it was just the steady sound of his breath and the rhythm of his shoes against the pavement.

When he slowed to a jog in front of the Airbnb again, sweat clung to the back of his neck, rolling down between his shoulder blades. His pulse beat steadily in his ears.

Inside, the shower still steamed behind him, fog clinging to the mirror as he raked a hand through his damp hair.

In the kitchen, the low churn of the blender filled the quiet, almond milk and frozen bananas whirling into something that looked healthier than he felt.

He leaned against the counter, the glass cool in his hand, taking slow sips.

The run had cleared his head, just not of her.

He settled at the small wooden table near the kitchen window overlooking Pine Hill's quiet streets. His laptop was open, but the inbox wasn't screaming at him the way it usually did.

A single note from his agent:

"No calls this week. Holiday break."

Sullivan smirked. That man knew better than to ruin Thanksgiving with contract talk.

He reached for his phone almost without thinking. A habit. Muscle memory.

No new messages. No missed calls.

No Brandy.

He hadn't expected a full conversation, but some part of him hoped she'd texted. Something small. A "good morning." A meme. Anything.

But he couldn't shake the way her laugh wrapped around him, a warmth he hadn't realized he needed. He typed before he could overthink it.

Sullivan: *Good morning*

The little "delivered" bubble blinked back at him, and then almost instantly, three dots appeared.

Brandy: *Morning*

He stared at the screen for a second, then grinned like a fool. Too fast. Too easy. She'd answered.

Sullivan: *Still good for 5pm?*

Brandy: *Yep. still down.*

Something loosened in his chest.

He hesitated only a second before typing again.

Sullivan: *Can I call you?*

Her reply came a breath later.

Brandy: *Yeah.*

He hit the call button.

Her voice came through soft but steady, wrapped in that familiar mix of calm and quiet humor that had always belonged to her. Something in him, something restless, finally settled.

"Hey," she said.

"What's up?" he answered, too quickly. Sullivan leaned back in his chair, eyes on the ceiling like it could steady him. "Just... wanted to check in. Make sure you were okay after our coffee date. And..." He exhaled, letting himself take the risk. "Wanted to hear your voice again."

There was a beat, a soft breath on the line.

"Oh," she said, her tone dipping warm, playful. "So you couldn't wait a few more hours to hear my voice? Should I be flattered?"

His smile pulled slow.

"Maybe."

"Maybe?" she echoed, the flirt tucked neatly into her laugh. "Well... lucky for you, I didn't mind hearing from you either."

Sullivan's breath caught, subtle but real. That one line landed right under his ribs, warming places he'd been afraid to look at too closely. He didn't say anything for a second, just let the quiet stretch, easy and full. His grin rose slow, unhurried, like he finally let himself feel all of it instead of pretending he didn't.

"Yeah," he murmured. "That's... good to know."

The conversation drifted easily after that, slipping back into something familiar. They joked about Ryan's over-the-top decorations and how she probably had personalized name cards and three different cider flavors. Brandy snorted when Sullivan admitted Jackson had already sent him at least three memes that morning. And of course, Desiree came up, because if trouble had a spokesperson, it would be her. Brandy's laughter came soft at first, then unguarded, filling the space between them like sunlight. It tugged at the corners of his mouth until he was laughing too, the quiet house around him fading into nothing.

"Wait," he said, still smiling. "I need a fit check."

She let out a playful groan, and the FaceTime ring filled the air a beat later.

When she answered, the screen jolted around for a second before settling on him in front of the mirror. He tilted the phone just enough to show off the dark green sweater stretched across his chest, dark jeans, brown boots, and that same Carhartt beanie she'd seen him in at the maze.

She leaned closer to the camera, mock-serious, like she was inspecting him. "Okay," she drawled, dragging the word out. "You clean up nice, Mr. Harper."

"Just nice?" He arched a brow at the screen.

Her lips curved into a grin. "Don't push it. You pass."

He pressed a hand to his chest like she'd wounded him. "Wow. High praise."

She laughed again, shaking her head, curls bouncing around her face.

"Fine," she added with a sly smile. "You look good."

The way she said it wasn't loud or dramatic, it was soft, like a secret that slipped out before she could catch it.

"Yeah?" His grin deepened, easy but gentle.

"Of course," she said, trying, and failing at not to sound too pleased.

The call ended with lingering smiles and a spark he couldn't quite name. He set his phone down and exhaled slowly, the house no less quiet, but somehow it didn't feel as empty anymore.

Chapter 11

The turkey was not cooperating. Ryan leaned over the roasting pan like it had personally disrespected her. "You better not play with me today," she muttered, basting brush in hand. "I have followers watching."

Her phone was propped on the counter, ring light glowing, livestream rolling. A hundred little red hearts floated up the screen as she narrated every move like she was hosting her own holiday special.

"Okay y'all," she said into the camera, flashing that polished influencer smile. "If you really want your turkey to be moist, the secret is..."

The oven timer beeped. Her phone vibrated. Something clattered in the sink behind her.

Ryan let out a short, unfiltered laugh. "The secret is not losing your mind while you do fifteen things at once."

The kitchen smelled like cinnamon and sage, a mix of baking pies and the cornbread dressing she'd prepped the night before. Platters lined the counters in neat rows. Copper mugs waited on a tray. A playlist of old-school soul and smooth holiday jazz filled the house.

It looked like something out of a Hallmark movie.

It also looked like someone had robbed a craft store.

"Alright, friends," Ryan said, holding up the baster like a microphone. "Moment of transparency? I might be losing it slightly. But it's fine. I've trained for this. I was born to host."

From the island, Chef Pierre, broad-shouldered and somewhere in his fifties, with a honey-thick Louisiana drawl stirred the pot of gumbo like he had all the time in the world. "Baby, you ain't losin' your mind," he said without looking up. "You're just entertainin' the masses. And this ain't even the stressful part yet."

Ryan pointed at him with the baster. "Pierre, you were supposed to reassure me."

"I am," he said, lifting the spoon for a taste. "This is me bein' supportive. Stress builds character."

She snorted. "Well, my character is built. I'd like peace now."

Chef Pierre chuckled, wiping his hands on a towel. "Mmm-hmm. And I'd like every pot in this kitchen to behave, but here we are."

Ryan leaned forward to end the livestream, smiling into the screen. "Love y'all. I'll post updates later. #FriendsgivingGoals #BlackGirlFall."

The second the stream ended, she blew out a dramatic breath and dropped the baster on the counter.

"Okay," she muttered, scanning the kitchen like a general surveying a battlefield. Turkey in the oven. Mac and cheese cooling. Sweet tea chilling. Bread rising. Decorations flawless. She'd even gotten matching napkin rings. Napkin rings.

Chef Pierre arched a brow. "Ryan, baby... you doin' the most."

"And I'll do it again," she said, snapping her fingers with conviction. Her phone dinged. A text from Brandy.

Brandy: *I'm getting ready now. Do you need anything else?*

Ryan: *Nope, I'm good. Don't forget to bring the sweet potato pies.*

Brandy: *rolling eyes emoji

Ryan grinned. That was Brandy's love language...sarcasm.

She spun around, adjusting the garland on the mantel. Fabian had been called in to the hospital at dawn, leaving her with the entire prep day solo. He'd promised he'd be home for dinner, but still, she missed the way he usually followed behind her, quietly doing all the heavy lifting while she did the "aesthetic" parts.

She brushed a stray curl behind her ear and looked around the living room. The space glowed: candles flickering, lights twinkling, warm cider scent drifting through the air.

This was what she'd wanted. All of them here. Together.

And with Sullivan back in town, the group would finally feel complete again.

"Alright," she whispered to herself, hands on her hips. "We're gonna make this perfect."

She moved from room to room, straightening pillows, lighting more candles, and fluffing blankets. She turned the music up just a little louder because, if she was going to stress clean, she was at least going to do it with a beat.

Outside, the morning sun poured through the big bay windows, catching the twinkling lights on the banister. Her dining table looked straight off Pinterest, rust-colored table runner, gold cutlery, tiny pumpkins scattered like confetti. Everyone had a place card and she strategically placed Sullivan and Brandy next to each other.

And if the day went exactly the way she'd planned...

They'd all be laughing around this table tonight, just like they used to.

Ryan paused near the window, wiping her hands on a dishtowel. The house was quiet except for the steady soft rumble of the oven and Donny Hathaway crooning through the speakers. For the first time all morning, she let herself breathe.

Her phone buzzed again. This time, it wasn't Brandy.

Fabian: *Surgery ran long. Should be home around five. Save me some mac & cheese.*

Ryan smiled, the tension in her shoulders loosening just a little.

Ryan: *You know I made a double batch. But if you're late, I'm hiding a plate.*

Fabian: *Love you, woman. Don't stress too much.*

A gentle ease settled in her chest. Fabian wasn't the grand gesture type. He was the quiet anchor who always made her laugh when she spun herself into a perfectionist storm.

She glanced at the long table one more time, twinkling lights catching the edge of the gold cutlery, cider scent curling through the air.

Ryan: *love you too. hurry home.*

She locked the screen, pressed the phone against her chest for half a second, then blew out a breath.

"Alright," she whispered to herself, straightening the centerpiece like the day depended on it. "Let's make this perfect."

Chapter 12

Brandy smoothed her hands down her forest-green sweater dress and let out a slow breath. The fabric hugged her softly, warm against her skin. She leaned closer to the mirror, adjusting the thin gold chain at her collarbone until it rested exactly right. Her curls framed her face in loose spirals that fell perfectly when she didn't overthink it.

She stared at her reflection for a long moment.

"Tonight is for you," she whispered. "Not him."

The ache Dante left behind still lingered somewhere deep, but she wasn't about to let it dictate her night. Not anymore.

She grabbed the two sweet potato pies from the counter. They were still warm, wrapped in soft kitchen towels to keep the heat in. They smelled like butter, cinnamon, and nutmeg. Like holidays. Like home. Like the recipe her grandmother Emily passed down.

Outside, a low hum of music drifted through the door. Sullivan's car idled in the driveway, headlights casting a soft amber glow over the street. He stepped out before she could even reach the car, his camel coat catching the porch light.

Forest-green crew-neck sweater. Dark jeans. A gold chain glinting against his skin. He looked 90s Love Jones fine. And then there was the smile, the one that made her heart skip without warning.

"Wow," he said with a soft laugh, eyes sweeping over her in a way that made heat rise to her cheeks. "Damn, girl. You look good. Shoot, we look good!"

She looked at her outfit, then at his. Both wearing forest green and camel. Completely in sync. A laugh rose up without warning.

"Yeah, we really do clean up nice," she said, lowering her gaze with a shy smile.

He opened the passenger door, still smiling. "Tell me that isn't a sign."

"A sign for what?" she teased as he closed the door behind her.

He circled around to the driver's side, slid in, and gave her a sideways grin. "A sign that we should be together." Then he broke into laughter, easing the air between them.

She shifted the pies in her lap, trying to hide her smile.

He grabbed his phone. "Wait, wait. Listen to this."

The smooth voice of Muni Long spilled through the speakers: *Twin, where have you been? Nobody knows you like I do.*

He sang along; eyebrows raised in mock seriousness.

"Oh Lord," Brandy burst out laughing. "Stop it!"

He turned the volume down, laughing too. "Hey, I'm just saying—we twinning tonight."

"Ha ha. Very funny."

"Okay, okay," he said, putting the car in drive. "Let's go before your pies get cold." He slid the boxes gently onto the back seat, his touch careful, deliberate.

They pulled onto the road, the heater blowing warm air into the quiet. The scent of cinnamon, brown sugar, and sweet potato lingered between them.

"So," Sullivan said, glancing over with that easy grin, "about those sweet potato pies..."

"I just know they taste even better than they smell."

Brandy's fingers tightened lightly around her seatbelt. She didn't have to look fully at him to feel the warmth rolling off his voice.

"You're already calling dibs?" she asked.

"Absolutely." He rested his arm on the console, angled slightly toward her. "I expect the first bite."

She tucked a curl behind her ear, stealing her own glance his way. "Well," she murmured, letting the playfulness show, "you might just get it."

He grinned wider, satisfied. "Good. I like a promise."

The dashboard cast a soft amber glow over his profile, warming the line of his jaw, the curl at the corner of his mouth. Every time he shifted, the air stirred with the faint mix of warm spice and cedarwood, the kind of scent that made you lean just a little closer without realizing it.

She could feel him glancing at her; quick, light, enough to make her pulse skip. He didn't comment on the way she kept fidgeting or how her breath caught when their eyes met for a second too long. Instead, his smile curved slow, like he understood more than he was saying. Like he wasn't in a rush to make anything happen. Like he had time... and didn't mind waiting for her heart to catch up.

Soft R&B hummed through the speakers as they drove.

By the time they turned onto Ryan's street, the house was already glowing. Twinkle lights wrapped around the porch railings. Candles flickered in the windows. A fall-themed wreath hung on the door. The scene looked like it had been pulled straight out of a movie.

Ryan's voice spilled out the second the door opened. "Ayyyyyy! My two favorite people are here!"

Brandy rolled her eyes, pretending she didn't feel that little shift inside.

"Wait...did y'all come together?!" Ryan squealed.

Brandy hugged her, shooting her a silent "girl, not now" look.

Ryan stood there in a burnt-orange apron with Grateful & Gorgeous across it in gold letters. With a glass of wine in hand, cheeks flushed with holiday joy. "Y'all cute or whatever," she declared, snatching the pies like a prize. "We are gonna have some fuuuun!"

Sullivan shot Brandy a small grin as they stepped over the threshold together, their coats brushing. Their hands grazed lightly. It wasn't intentional. But the way everyone looked at them... it might as well have been.

And for the first time in a long time, Brandy didn't have to fake a smile.

It was genuine.
Standing next to Sullivan didn't feel like a performance.
It felt safe.
It felt real.

Chapter 13

The second Brandy and Sullivan stepped inside Ryan's house, the smell of cinnamon, roasted turkey, and sweet glaze wrapped around them like a hug.

The living room was exactly what Brandy expected from Ryan, too much in all the best ways.

Twinkle lights wound around the banisters. Oversized plaid pillows crowded the couch. A crackling fire flickered in the stone fireplace. The dining table was already set like something straight out of a Hallmark movie, layered runners, name cards, miniature pumpkins, and candles glowing low.

"Lord," Sullivan muttered beside her. "She went all out."

"She always does," Brandy whispered back, biting back a laugh.

"Y'all hush and respect my vision!" Ryan called from the kitchen; hair tucked into a cute beret. She moved around like a woman hosting a national broadcast special. Fabian stood behind her in a matching sweater, because of course they coordinated. He was waiting for orders like he was her sous chef.

"Hey, family!" Jackson's voice boomed from the doorway as he and Gabby stepped in.

Gabby looked like autumn personified, hooded burgundy duffle coat, honey-colored locs peeking from under her beanie, a cloud of patchouli and sage following her. Jackson had his arm draped over her shoulders, tall and lean, his grin wide enough to light up the room.

"Boy, it smells like heaven up in here," Jackson said, sniffing the air. "I'm about to grab a plate right now."

Fabian shot him a look over the counter. "You try it, and you gon' lose a hand."

77

Sullivan laughed. "Man, you still guarding food like you did in college cookouts?"

Fabian grinned. "And I still don't trust y'all around my rolls."

Everyone cracked up as Ryan set down a tray of appetizers.

"Okay, okay, introductions before y'all act up. This is my cousin Jaz and her wife, Aerianna. They're visiting from Portland!"

Jaz waved, her plum-colored sweater slipping off one shoulder, gold bangles clinking as she smiled.

"Hey, y'all. This spread looks like something out of Pinterest. I'm impressed."

"Pinterest?" Ryan gasped. "Ma'am, this is pure Black Girl Magic. Handmade and hand-curated."

Aerianna laughed, already vibing with the guys near the TV. "Alright, but where the football at?"

Before Fabian could answer, Jaz's eyes suddenly widened, laser-focused on Sullivan.

"Wait... hold on." She grabbed Aerianna's arm. "Is that Sullivan Harper? Like... the Sullivan Harper?"

Aerianna snorted. "Lord, here we go. Babe, his books are the only reason I ever get time on the PS5. Every time he drops a new one, you disappear for two days."

Jaz shot her a playful glare. "And I will do it again. That man writes romance like he's trying to ruin my marriage in the best way."

Sullivan laughed, rubbing the back of his neck, embarrassed but trying to be polite.

"I promise I am not trying to ruin anything. But it's nice to meet you."

Jaz practically melted.

"Oh my God... would you sign my copy later? I legit brought you newest book 'If This World Were Mine' with me. It's in the car."

Sullivan's smile turned shy and genuine.

"Of course. Just let me know when."

Aerianna nudged Jaz. "See? Look at you. Try not to faint before dessert."

Fabian turned the football on immediately. "Uhhh, anyway. Girl, I got you. Cowboys playing right now. Grab a plate."

Moments later, the front door swung open like it owed somebody money. Desiree stepped in first, chin high, hips switching, Chicago stamped all over her entrance. She didn't even pause. She scanned the room, hair laid, makeup flawless, and tossed her coat onto the nearest chair like she owned the lease.

Brandy didn't even have time to fully inhale before Dez pulled her into a hug that was half affection, half headlock.

"Girl, why you standing here like somebody's sad auntie?" Desiree muttered into her ear, then kissed her cheek like she hadn't just dragged her.

Behind her, Marcus followed, tall, fine, and radiating pure regret. The only time his face lit up was when he spotted the football game on the TV.

"It smells so good in here! I can't wait to eat!" Desiree announced, already setting her purse down and strutting straight to the bar. "Ryan, girl, you are doing the absolute most."

Ryan laughed. Brandy shook her head, smiling despite herself.

This was Desiree, unapologetic, loud love wrapped in a Chicago attitude and perfect eyebrows. "You're welcome," Ryan shot back, arranging charcuterie boards across the table. "Me casa su casa, people! Dinner is about an hour away, so snack, sip, and stay out of my kitchen."

The house stirred with the energy only old friends could bring. Everyone talking over each other, laughter bouncing off the walls, music blending with football commentary. Someone had already started a spades game at the dining room table, and trash talk filled the air.

Brandy was still grinning when she slipped into the kitchen. The air was warmer there, thick with the scent of brown sugar glaze and roasted meat. She reached for a serving fork, glancing over her shoulder to make sure Ryan wasn't around. She was starving and just wanted a little taste of the ham.

"You need help with anything?"

The voice came from behind her, low, smooth, and unhurried.

She jumped slightly, turning toward him. "Shh," she whispered, hand over her chest. "I'm trying to sneak a piece of this ham."

Sullivan leaned against the doorframe, the corner of his mouth curling. "Caught red-handed."

"I know," she said, fighting a smile. "Ryan'll kill me if she catches me."

He chuckled softly, eyes never leaving her. "Alright, I got you. I'll be your lookout. Go on, get your slice."

Brandy laughed under her breath, her voice barely above a whisper. "You're ridiculous."

"Maybe," he said, "but I'm loyal."

Ryan's shout echoed from the living room, something about the Cowboys scoring and Sullivan used it as cover, turning his head toward the noise like a real lookout.

Brandy carved off a small bite, the fork clinking softly against the dish. She popped it into her mouth and closed her eyes for a second, savoring it, the salt, the sweetness, a slow comfort unfolding inside her. When she opened her eyes again, Sullivan was watching her.

No easy grin. No polite distance. His eyes stayed on her, steady, like he'd lost the thread of why he walked in. Her breath hitched. The air between them went still, heavy with everything neither of them said.

His gaze dropped briefly to her mouth, quick, almost imperceptible, then back up to her eyes. The move was small but deliberate, and Brandy's pulse betrayed her, fluttering against her throat like it was trying to escape.

She tried to break the moment with humor. "You're not gonna tell on me, right?"

"Not a chance." His voice was low, but there was something underneath it, something warm and rough that made her toes curl in her boots. "Besides," he said, leaning a little closer, "you looked too happy just now. I wouldn't ruin that."

Brandy blinked, heat crawling up her neck. She laughed softly, a nervous, quiet sound. "Thanks for not snitching."

"Anytime," he said and this time, his tone dropped enough that she could feel it more than hear it.

Their eyes lingered, suspended in that hush before the noise from the rest of the house rushed back in, laughter, clinking glasses.

Brandy turned away first, pretending to straighten a dish. But her hands trembled just enough that she had to grip the counter to steady herself.

And when she finally looked up again, Sullivan was still watching her, a slow smile playing at his lips like he knew exactly what he'd just done to her.

"Alright!" Ryan's voice broke the moment. "Let's play a quick game before we eat!"

Jackson groaned. "Please tell me it's not charades again."

"Nope!" Ryan said, producing a bowl of folded cards. "Friendsgiving Trivia, baby! Made it myself!"

"Oh Lord," Desiree muttered, already fixing her drink.

Sullivan leaned in, close enough that Brandy felt the warmth of him before she heard him. His breath grazed the shell of her ear, low and teasing.

"I'm betting she rigged it."

Her laugh slipped out softer than she meant, caught somewhere between a whisper and a sigh. "Of course she did."

She tried to look away, but his nearness pulled at her attention like gravity. He hadn't moved yet, and the air between them grew charged quiet, electric, alive.

Brandy felt her pulse climb, steady and sure beneath the surface. His scent lingered near her, close enough to catch. And for a heartbeat, the laughter softened into something quiet and real.

Ryan divided everyone into teams: Brandy, Sullivan, Gabby, and Cousin Jaz versus Jackson, Desiree, Aerianna, and Marcus. Fabian played referee, already shaking his head.

"Alright," Ryan said dramatically. "Team One y'all up first. Which Thanksgiving dish automatically gets disqualified if the cook doesn't season it?"

A. Mac and cheese

B. Greens

C. Turkey

D. All of the above

Jaz shot her hand up fast, bangles jingling. "Ooh! I know this one!"

"Okay, cousin, what you got?" Ryan said, smirking.

"Greens!" Jaz said, beaming.

Her team erupted. "Good answer! Good answer!" Sullivan clapped, hyping her up like they were on Family Feud.

Ryan grinned. "Wrong!"

"Now how that's wrong?" Gabby yelled.

"Told you she rigged it," Sullivan whispered to Brandy, who was laughing too hard to breathe.

Jackson shook his head. "Yo, Ryan, this wild."

Ryan held the card high. "The answer is D, all of 'em. Because y'all know better!"

The room exploded in laughter.

"Next question!" Fabian called, shuffling the cards. "Finish this sentence: You can't trust everybody's ____ at Thanksgiving."

A. Greens

B. Potato salad

C. Turkey

D. Sweet tea

Before anyone could answer, Marcus blurted out, "Sweet tea!"

The room fell silent, then burst into chaos.

Desiree covered her face, laughing. "It's okay, baby! You right, can't trust everybody's sweet tea."

Marcus blinked, confused. "Wait, what is it then?"

Everyone yelled in unison, "Potato salad!"

Aerianna shook her head. "Duh, man!"

The whole room howled. Ryan was doubled over laughing, crying into her napkin.

Sullivan watched her, the way her laughter folded into the room, easy, unguarded, and alive. Her shoulders shook, cheeks flushed, eyes bright beneath the soft golden light.

For the first time in a long while, she looked weightless. Like the world had finally let her breathe.

And something in him ached at the sight.

He could do this every year, he realized. Sit in rooms like this. Watch her laugh like that.

He'd missed too many of these nights...too many chances to feel what real life actually felt like.

Eventually, Ryan clapped her hands. "Okay, now that y'all burned some calories slapping fives and hollering, it's time to eat!"

She herded everyone into the dining room. "As you'll see, there's a seating arrangement. Find your name, take your seat, and yes, I planned it."

As everyone found their spots, Chef Pierre entered in a white chef's coat and hat.

Ryan grinned. "I'd like y'all to meet Chef Pierre. He'll be serving us tonight."

Desiree's eyes went wide. "Now wait a damn minute! I thought you said you cooked all this yourself?"

Laughter rippled through the table.

Ryan put on her best debutante accent. "Darling, I never said I cooked anything. I curated the experience."

The group cracked up as Chef Pierre presented the first dishes. Plates piled high. Wine poured freely. The sound of forks, laughter, and love filled every corner of the house.

Jackson cracked jokes between bites. Ryan narrated the meal like she was on a cooking show. Gabby kept everyone's glasses full.

Somewhere between the laughter, the clinking of glasses, and the soft glow of candlelight, Brandy caught him looking at her again.

Sullivan sat across the table, thanks to Ryan's not-so-subtle "strategic" seating and for a moment, the noise around them fell away.

His gaze wasn't heavy, just steady. Curious. Familiar. It landed on her like a touch.

Brandy took a slow breath. Her fingers brushed the stem of her wine glass, holding onto the coolness there as something shifted in her. She didn't look away this time.

The candlelight flickered between them, soft and golden, catching in the rim of his glass and the small smile tugging at his lips.

For a breath, it felt like the table, the laughter, the world itself, all of it tilted toward that quiet space between them.

And Brandy thought, Lord, don't let me fall too fast.

Chapter 14

Brandy's laughter had settled into a soft hush under her breath as the chatter around the table carried on. She could still feel Sullivan's gaze, steady, quiet, burning at the edges of her composure.

And that was exactly why she needed to get up.

Her pulse tripped as she stood, smoothing her dress, forcing a polite smile when Ryan teased about "dessert duties." Truth was, she just needed a moment to breathe. To think.

Or maybe to stop thinking.

The kitchen was cozy, still glowing with the soft aftermath of dinner. The air smelled like cinnamon, nutmeg, and roasted sugar. She exhaled and opened the oven, pulling out the two sweet potato pies she'd kept warm. Grandma Emily's recipe. Her legacy, her love. No fancy chef was stealing credit for that.

Behind her, the door creaked.

"I thought I'd find you in here," Sullivan said, voice low, velvet smooth.

Brandy turned, nearly dropping the pie server. "Lord, you scared me."

He leaned against the counter, hands in his pockets, that familiar teasing curve in his smile. "Couldn't let you sneak dessert without me. Remember, I've got first dibs."

Her lips curved despite herself. "I remember."

"Good." His eyes softened, catching the glow of the kitchen lights. "Because I've been thinking about that pie all night."

She laughed quietly, cutting him a slice. "You've been thinking about food?"

His gaze lingered. "Not exactly."

Her hand trembled just enough to make the fork clink against the plate. She passed it to him, but he didn't take it.

"Uh-uh," he said softly, voice dropping. "You promised me the first bite, remember?"

Her breath caught. "I...did I?"

He stepped closer. "Guess we're about to find out."

The space between them folded. Brandy swallowed hard, her pulse thudding somewhere near her throat. Slowly, she lifted the fork, cut into the pie, and held it out to him.

Sullivan didn't rush. He leaned in, eyes never leaving hers, his hand brushing hers just enough to spark something electric. When he took the bite, his lips grazed the fork, slow and deliberate.

"Mm," he said softly, voice rougher now. "Sweet."

Her heart stuttered. She tried to laugh it off, but the sound caught in her chest.

Then he looked at her, really looked at her and whatever distance they'd been pretending to keep dissolved.

He grabbed her waist, gently, the warmth of his body blending with hers in a quiet, steady pull toward him.

It happened slowly, like the world was waiting for it.

When his lips met hers, it wasn't hungry. It wasn't rushed. It was soft and sure, like something that had been waiting its turn for years. The kiss deepened in a slow, warm sweep, sweet enough to make her chest flutter, sensual in the way his breath brushed hers between each unhurried second.

The taste of sweet potato and brown sugar lingered between them. When they finally broke apart, the air felt different, thicker, alive with something neither of them named.

Sullivan's forehead rested against hers, his breath still catching. "Worth the wait," he murmured.

Brandy smiled, cheeks flushed, voice barely above a whisper. "Which part?"

He grinned. "All of it."

Brandy was still smiling when the sound of laughter drifted in from the dining room. The spell loosened, but not completely. It hung between them, sweet and quiet, like the cinnamon still perfuming the air.

Sullivan brushed his thumb against her hand before stepping back.

"You should probably get that pie out there before Ryan comes looking for us."

Brandy laughed, breath still unsteady. "You're right. She'll have a whole fit if she thinks we're hiding in here."

He smirked, grabbing the second pie for her. "Yeah, let's not give her a reason to come shut the kitchen down."

They walked back into the dining room, slipping into the warmth of music and laughter. Ryan was dancing with a wine glass like she was auditioning for a holiday commercial, Jackson was yelling about a Spades rematch, and Desiree was already halfway to the bar for a refill.

Nobody noticed right away that Brandy's cheeks were still flushed, or that Sullivan couldn't stop smiling.

But Ryan noticed everything.

She froze, mid two-step, eyebrow lifting in slow suspicion.

"Why do y'all look like y'all been up to something?"

Brandy shot her a quick, playful look. "Just serving dessert."

Ryan raised her glass, smirking. "Mmhmm. Well, whatever kind of dessert that was, it looks good on both of y'all."

The room erupted into laughter, teasing rolling in easy and warm. Sullivan shook his head, chuckling under his breath as Brandy set the pies on the table.

And instantly

"Awww yeah, that's Brandy's sweet potato pie," Fabian announced. "I've been waiting on this all night."

Jackson clapped once, loud. "Move. I need the first slice. I been preparing my spirit for this."

Gabby fanned the air dramatically. "Sis... the smell alone? Bless you."

Desiree held her plate out like communion. "Don't nobody speak to me until I get mine."

The room buzzed with joy and noise, wrapping around Brandy like home.

Across the table, Sullivan watched her with that soft, unguarded smile again.

And she felt it.

Sweet, steady, humming through her chest like something she wasn't afraid to feel anymore.

Dinner plates were quickly traded for dessert and comfortable seating. The crew drifted into the living room, settling onto couches and chairs as the music softened into a slow groove. Brandy found a spot on the couch, and Jaz slipped in beside her, legs crossed, eyes already bright with curiosity.

"Okay, wait," Jaz said, lifting her wine glass like a mic. "I've been dying to ask this all night. Where is everybody from, and how did y'all end up here together? This group feels... so close."

Fabian snorted. "Translation: she's nosy."

"Very," Aerianna added, sipping from her copper mug.

"Alright, I'll start," Desiree said, flipping her hair over her shoulder and kicking her feet up like she was centerstage. "I'm from Chicago. Born and raised. Met Brandy freshman year at Hampton. We were both psych majors and inseparable."

"And you can't tell by the way they stay at each other's throats," Jackson chimed in.

"Oh, shut up, Jack!" Desiree snapped. The group cackled.

"Oh! She called him Jack! Ain't heard that in a while!" Ryan wheezed.

"Anyway," Desiree continued, turning to Jaz, "me and Brandy were already cool. Then we met Ry. She was our RA. And we were like Destiny's Child."

The group hollered. Then immediately, Ryan and Dez said at the same time, "I'm Beyoncé!"

Jackson, the clown of the group, was in tears. Sullivan nearly choked on his drink. Everyone else was fully gone with laughter.

"Heaux, you ain't no damn Beyoncé," Ryan laughed, shoving Dez playfully.

"Okay, fine. I'm Kelly," Dez conceded, rolling her eyes. They laughed harder, and Brandy sighed dramatically.

"And I've always been the Michelle of the group."

Something about the way she said it sent the whole room into another wave of laughter.

"Okay, okay, let me finish," Dez said, fanning herself. "Jaz wanna know the story."

Jaz nodded, fully entertained.

"So, we met these three" Dez pointed at Sullivan, Fabian, and Jackson. "At the kickbacks we used to have in the dorms." She settled onto Marcus's lap like she'd been waiting for that seat all night.

"But I only stayed till junior year. Psychology was not my thing. I had to go."

Brandy laughed. "Girl, you left so fast."

"Sure did," Dez said proudly. "I went back home thinking I was gonna thrive in the city. Nope. Chicago humbled me real quick. So, I packed my bags, came right back to Pine Hill, went to beauty school in Richmond, did makeup out my little apartment downtown for a minute... which YES, included that last-minute job for that rap duo everybody swears is cousins."

"Oh Lord..." Jackson groaned. "Here she go."

"Yes, here I go!" Dez snapped her fingers. "And now I own my shop. Period."

Everyone clapped as she lifted her wine glass in a little 'cheers' motion.

Jackson slung an arm around the back of Gabby's chair. "I'm from Houston. Did law school here in Virginia, met Gabby courtesy of Van, and I wasn't about to leave her fine self behind."

Gabby swatted him playfully. "Boy, hush."

"What? It's true," he said, grinning. "Man chooses love over heatstroke. I don't miss Houston summers even a little."

Jaz nodded approvingly. "Okay, romantic lawyer. I see you."

Brandy raised her hand. "I'm from Minneapolis. Minnesota born and frozen."

The whole room burst out laughing.

Jackson wiped an imaginary tear. "You are the only Black person from Minnesota I've ever met."

"Right!?" Dez chimed in. "When we met freshman year, she said 'bayg,' and I had to ask her to repeat it like three times. Ma'am, are you saying BAG? Like B-A-G, bag? Girl drove me crazy."

The group hollered again.

"She exaggerated her A's on everything," Sullivan added.

Brandy rolled her eyes, laughing. "Anyway. I stayed because I hate the cold and I love my job here."

"Amen," Ryan said. "Speaking of staying, me, and Fabian? We've been together since freshman year. I was a marketing major and he started his medical rotations in the area, and I was not about to be somebody's long-distance girlfriend. So, Pine Hill it was."

Fabian shrugged. "Plus, Ryan decorated the apartment once, and I was trapped."

Ryan slapped his shoulder. "You're welcome."

All eyes shifted to Sullivan.

Jaz leaned forward, chin in her hand. "Alright, mister bestselling author. Your turn."

He laughed, rubbing the back of his neck, that little tell he always had. "Well, I'm from here. My momma still lives in the same house I grew up in. College was right down the road for me. I grew up with Gabby."

"Yeah, we're practically cousins," Gabby added with a laugh.

"But yeah," Sullivan continued, "I was an English major at Hampton. Ran track. I didn't really stay... been living in New York for about the last decade."

Ryan snorted. "Translation: he was not trying to stay in this small town after college."

"Also true," Sullivan admitted, smiling.

"What made you write romance?" Jaz asked, eyes wide.

He hesitated, gaze flicking briefly toward Brandy.

"I've always loved stories about love... Black love specifically," he said. "About people showing up for each other. My first book was about that. 'Innocent Love' was about a young college couple trying to figure themselves out."

Dez blinked slowly, then grinned like the devil himself handed her the line.

"Now hold on." She pointed dramatically between them. "Van... be honest. That story was about you and Braaaannddddyyyy."

She stretched Brandy's name out like warm taffy.

The room exploded in laughter.

"Now you know that book was not about me!" Brandy said, face blazing, hands covering her cheeks.

Sullivan chuckled, rubbing the back of his neck again, completely giving himself away.

"Uhhh... nah."

Jackson slung an arm around him. "It was about Sheronda! You know, Sheronda with the bubble butt!"

Gabby smacked him across the head. "Shut up, fool!"

More laughter erupted. Even Sullivan bent over, shaking his head.

Brandy didn't look at him right away.

When she finally did, Sullivan was already watching her soft, steady and something unspoken warming behind his eyes.

The chatter swirled around them, loud and happy.

But between the jokes and the pie and the glow of candlelight, something in the room shifted...quiet, delicate, real.

Brandy felt it.

He felt it too.

And suddenly, running didn't feel like the only option anymore.

Chapter 15

Sullivan hadn't stopped smiling all night. The laughter. The food. The warmth. It felt like coming home to something he didn't even realize he'd been missing. And sitting here now on Ryan's overstuffed loveseat, next to Brandy he couldn't imagine being anywhere else.

She was close enough that he could smell her perfume; something soft and sweet like vanilla and clove. Her curls brushed his shoulder every time she turned to laugh, and that tiny sound of hers, a half giggle, and half sigh, had already burned itself into his memory. He caught her looking at him again, that same dazed, curious spark she'd had in the kitchen. It made his chest tighten in a way he couldn't laugh off this time.

"So..." she started, eyes fixed on the glass she was turning slowly in her hands. "What was that?"

He tilted his head, playing innocent. "What was what?"

"You know," she said, finally glancing up at him. "You kissed me in the kitchen."

Sullivan's mouth curved, slow and knowing. "Well, if I recall, you kissed me back."

She laughed soft and low, shaking her head. "Oh, here you go."

"Nah, all jokes aside..." His voice dropped, losing its teasing edge. "The moment just felt right, Bran. I didn't want to let the night pass without you knowing how I feel."

Her laughter faded. The world seemed to quiet again.

"Sullivan..." she said, his name barely above a whisper.

He leaned in just a little, close enough that she could feel the warmth of his breath. "You don't have to say anything. I just needed you to know."

Brandy's pulse fluttered in her throat. "You're making this hard," she murmured, eyes dipping to his lips before she caught herself.

He grinned softly. "Good."

Their quiet moment broke when Desiree's voice cut through the low chatter of conversation.

"Nah, let me whoop y'all heads real quick in Uno!" she shouted, already shuffling cards like a Vegas dealer.

Jackson groaned from across the room. "Man, you only win cause you make up your own rules!"

"Boy, please," Desiree shot back. "That's called strategy."

The room erupted into laughter. Aerianna slid a chair up to the card table, rolling up her sleeves. "Let me get in on that."

Her wife Jaz side-eyed her. "Babe, you know how serious you get at Uno."

"I promise just one game," Aerianna said, crossing her heart. "I won't even cause no trouble."

"Mmhm," Jaz muttered. "That's what you said last time."

Ryan floated through the chaos, wine glass in hand, snapping a quick picture of the table. Fabian stood behind her, smiling as she leaned in and kissed his cheek. "Thank you," she mouthed to him, a little gesture of gratitude for helping her pull off a perfect Friendsgiving.

The house glowed with comfort. Gabby was half asleep on one end of the sofa, Jackson and Desiree were talking trash over cards, and Brandy felt that quiet sense of belonging press against her ribs. Sullivan's arm brushed hers as he reached for his drink, and she couldn't help the small smile that followed.

Then

A knock.

Loud. Sharp. Unexpected.

The laughter hiccupped to silence. Everyone froze for a beat, glancing toward the door.

Ryan frowned. "Now who is that knocking on my door like they're the police?"

Fabian laughed nervously, setting his drink down. "Maybe Chef Pierre forgot his hat."

They both walked toward the door, still smiling as Ryan pulled it open and froze.

Standing there, bouquet of grocery store roses in hand, was Dante. "Dante?!"

Ryan and Fabian said it at the same time, like the name itself knocked the air out of the room.

There he was, deep brown skin, that beard she used to trace with her thumb, that smile that could make her melt like butter on sweet bread. A smile that made forgetting easier than forgiving.

His presence hit the room like perfume, familiar, disarming, dangerous.

Brandy's glass slipped from her hand, the sip she'd just taken spluttering back out as she coughed, eyes wide. The sound cracked through the silence.

Sullivan looked at her first. She'd gone still, shoulders tense, fingers trembling slightly on the rim of the glass. The color drained from her face as if her body had recognized the name before her mind could.

He shifted forward on the couch, every muscle on alert. "Bran?" he said softly, but she didn't hear him.

Before anyone else could move, Desiree shot up from the card table. Uno cards flew like confetti.

"Dante?! Hell, is you doing here?!" she barked, already storming toward the door. "I know damn well you didn't get an invite!"

"Well hello to you too, Dez," Dante said, voice smooth as glass. He stood there framed in the doorway, roses in one hand, confidence in the other. The faint scent of his cologne slipped into the house: soft spice and something darker. He looked good. Too good. Sullivan felt his jaw tighten.

Ryan stumbled over her words, eyes darting between Brandy and the door. "Wait, what are you doing here, Dante?"

Dante's grin didn't falter. He shifted the bouquet, the perfect picture of charm. "Well, I thought I'd surprise my baby, Brandy. And I thought I was invited."

"Well, the invite was rescinded when you did my girl dirty!" Desiree shot back, stepping closer until Marcus instinctively rose from his chair behind her. She glanced over her shoulder. "Brandy, you better come get rid of him before I have Marcus do it!"

Marcus cracked his neck like he was stretching for warm-ups.

Sullivan's pulse quickened. He wanted to move, and wanted to stand next to Brandy, to be a barrier but this wasn't his fight. Not yet.

Brandy blinked, finally snapping out of the fog. "I...I got it," she said quickly.

She pushed past Desiree her shoulder brushing Ryan's arm, not looking back. Sullivan caught the faint tremor in her hand as she passed him. The air around her shifted; the softness he'd seen all evening hardened into something he hadn't seen before- defense, or survival.

He started, but the front door was already swung close behind her.

Through the window, Sullivan saw Dante's posture tilt forward, voice low, steady, coaxing. Brandy's shoulders went tight, just a fraction. Sullivan didn't need to make out the words. He recognized that tone. Soft enough to pass as tenderness. Sharp enough to box someone in. Inside, Desiree was pacing, muttering under her breath. Jackson pretended to straighten the card pile, though his eyes were fixed on the door. Ryan just stood there, hands fluttering, torn between hostess and friend.

Fabian rubbed the back of his neck. "You want me to-?"

"No," Sullivan said quietly, still staring through the window. "Let her handle it."

He hoped she would.

He hoped she'd see through whatever speech Dante had come rehearsed with.

But when he saw Dante reach for her hand and Brandy didn't immediately pull away, something in Sullivan's chest twisted hard.

He looked down, gripping the edge of his glass until his knuckles went white. The room murmured with half-whispered commentary, but he didn't hear it. All he could think was how quickly peace could turn into noise.

Chapter 16

The night air hit her first, cold, sharp, almost cleansing. The laughter that once floated from inside Ryan's house was now muffled hushes and shuffling behind the closed door, like a life she'd just stepped out of.

Dante stood on the porch beneath the string lights, roses still in his hand, confidence worn like cologne. He looked almost the same; pressed coat, polished smile, eyes that once felt like home and now only reminded her what it cost.

"Brandy," he said, his voice low, careful. "You look beautiful."

She folded her arms. "Don't."

"Don't what?"

"Act like nothing happened."

A sigh spilled out of him, soft and deliberate. "I deserved that. But can you blame me for trying to see you? I miss you."

"Miss me?" she repeated, bitterness rising. "You ended our engagement over a text, Dante. You sent your mama to pick up your things like I was a bill you were done paying."

He winced, then nodded, stepping closer. The scent of vanilla and the cologne she once bought him reached her nose, and her chest tightened in all the old, dangerous ways.

"I panicked, Bran. That's all. Things got heavy, and I needed to breathe. But being away from you-" His voice cracked just slightly, perfectly rehearsed. "Made me realize I can't do this life without you."

Her throat worked around a lump she didn't want. "You can't just say that and expect everything to reset."

"I'm not expecting anything. I just want to talk. Please. You owe me that much."

That word...*owe*, landed like a weight.

Brandy stared at the roses, at his hands, at the ground between them. Old habits stirred.

"Five minutes," she said quietly.

A small, victorious smile ghosted across his face before he masked it. "That's all I need."

He reached for her hand. His palm was hot, heavy, and familiar.

And she didn't move.

Through the front window, she saw shadows; faces gathered inside, watching. Ryan's worried frown. Desiree's glare. Fabian's folded arms. Sullivan... standing still by the loveseat, unreadable. The flicker of candlelight glinted off his jaw, his shoulders squared tight.

Her stomach twisted.

She stepped back inside. The air shifted; conversation died on cue.

Desiree spoke first. "I know you not about to leave with him."

"Brandy, sweetheart," Ryan said, voice trembling. "You don't have to do this, baby. Not tonight."

Brandy forced a laugh that didn't sound like her at all. "I'm not doing anything. He just wants to talk. He's already here, might as well get it over with."

Fabian moved beside her, protective, calm. "If you want him gone, just say the word, baby sis."

She felt every eye on her, including Sullivan's. He hadn't said a thing, but his silence carried the loudest weight.

"I'm fine," she said quickly. "Really. Dante's gonna be Dante."

Desiree scoffed. "You mean manipulative, lying-"

"Dez," Ryan cut in, but the damage was done.

Brandy grabbed her coat and purse, each motion too fast, too practiced. She couldn't look at Sullivan, if she did, she'd unravel. Still, she could feel him behind her; that steady, quiet presence that had begun to mean safety.

She forced a smile she didn't feel. "I'll call y'all as soon as he's gone, okay?"

Ryan nodded, eyes glossy. Desiree just shook her head, muttering under her breath.

Brandy paused at the doorway. For a heartbeat, hope flickered maybe Sullivan would stop her. Maybe he'd reach for her hand, say her name the way he did in the kitchen, remind her that warmth could be real.

But he didn't move.

And she didn't turn around.

The door shut behind her, sealing the laughter, the light, the scent of sweet-potato pie inside.

OUT ON THE PORCH, DANTE was waiting at the curb, leaning against his car like he'd been there longer than he'd ever admitted.

Brandy exhaled, a sound somewhere between resolve and regret.

Then she walked toward him, the night swallowing her whole.

"You good?" he asked quietly.

Brandy wasn't. And for all their mess, Dante always knew when she wasn't.

She shook her head. "Dante, you shouldn't have come here tonight."

"I came because I care about us, baby. That should count for something."

He said.

Her mouth parted. "You showed up because you don't like looking like the bad guy."

"That's crazy," he scoffed. "You always twist stuff in your head. I'm the one trying here-you the one in there smiling in another man's face."

The emotional whiplash hit like a slap. Her stomach dropped.

"Dante, stop."

"Just say you're replacing me," he snapped. "Just say you done with me so I can stop looking stupid."

"You are the one that called off the engagement. You are the one that moved out of the apartment. Now I'm the one replacing you?" She huffed.

She shook her head, overwhelmed, chest hot and tight. "I can't do this out here. Not in front of—-"

"Then get in the car," he said, opening the door. "Let's talk like adults."

She should have walked away. She knew that.

But she was tired...bone-deep tired.

And when he looked at her, his voice softening just enough to mimic care, it tugged at old wounds she hadn't healed yet.

"Baby," he murmured, "just talk to me."

Her resolve crumbled.

She got in.

Not because she chose him.

Because she didn't trust herself to stand here one more minute without falling apart.

What followed was chaos, sharp words, long silences, his voice rising and falling, her throat burning. By the time they reached his new condo, she was exhausted, numb, and hurt emotionally.

He walked ahead of her without waiting.

And she followed up the stairs, through the hallway, into a life that no longer had space for her.

BRANDY BARELY HAD TIME to take in the bare walls and the cold, hotel-like silence of his new place before Dante was already pacing.

"So that's it?" he snapped, tossing his keys onto the counter. "You hang out with your little crew for one holiday and suddenly you're done with us?"

She blinked. "Done? Dante... you called off the engagement."

"Oh my God," he groaned, dragging a hand across his face. "Here you go bringing up old stuff."

"Old stuff?" Her voice cracked. "You told me I wasn't ready. You told me you weren't ready. And then you moved out without a conversation. Without a plan. You sent your mother to get your things like I was a stranger who needed to be handled."

He scoffed. "I needed space, Brandy. You were suffocating me."

Her breath hitched, the familiar sting of a wound he loved reopening.

"You went to the Poconos for a "boys' trip" the same weekend you said you needed space. And with another woman. How was I suffocating you from miles away?"

He stiffened but didn't break stride. "You don't know the whole story."

"I saw the pictures," she said quietly. "You didn't even hide it."

"That wasn't even like that," he snapped. "And you blowing it up is exactly why I needed time."

She stared at him, stunned. "Wow. You move out, you disappear, you take another woman on the trip with you, and somehow, I'm the problem?"

"I never said that." His voice softened instantly, a tone she'd heard too many times. "Baby, I just... I wasn't ready. Marriage is big. I freaked out. But that doesn't mean I don't love you."

Her stomach twisted. "Every time you say you love me, it comes after a lie."

He stepped toward her. "Come on, babe. Don't do that. You know you're my heart. I've just been under pressure. Work's been crazy. You been emotional... You make everything heavier than it needs to be."

There it was.

The spiral.

The twisting of her reality until she questioned her own.

"I'm emotional because you betrayed me," she said, voice shaking.

"Look," he said, palms up like he was being reasonable, "the Poconos thing was nothing. You really gonna throw away three years over that?"

"You threw it away," she whispered. "I just... stopped pretending you didn't."

He exhaled sharply, the softness gone again. "So, what, you with that dude now? Van? I saw your little picture together. That's what this is about, huh? You finally got you a backup?"

Her jaw clenched. "Don't do that."

"Then be honest," he fired back. "You feeling him? You gave up on us that fast?"

She swallowed hard, chest burning. "This isn't about him. This is about you. Calling off the engagement. The lies. The gaslighting. The way you made me feel like I imagined every red flag."

"You always exaggerate," he muttered. "Always looking for something wrong."

"No," she said, voice steadying, "I'm finally seeing things clearly."

He laughed, short and ugly. "Man... whatever. You always gonna need somebody to blame."

Her heart thudded, heavy, and tired. "Dante... I didn't come here for us to get back together. I came here because I needed to say what I never got to say. You left me. You checked out. And I was still trying to fix something you broke."

His expression cracked, anger, disbelief, pride all fighting for space. "So that's it?" he said quietly. "You really done with me?"

Brandy swallowed, because the truth hurt even when it freed her.

"I think I was done the day you left," she whispered.

For a long moment, neither of them moved.

Then the fight drained out of her body all at once, leaving only exhaustion in its place.

She sank onto the edge of the couch because her legs were shaking.

He kept talking, circling, deflecting, denying, promising, accusing and his voice rising and falling like it always did when he felt control slipping.

She didn't argue back. She didn't defend herself. She didn't have the strength.

At some point she leaned back. At some point her eyes drifted close.

At some point the chaos blurred into silence.

She fell asleep on his couch still wearing her coat.

Not out of comfort.

But because her body finally gave out long before her heart stopped hurting.

Chapter 17

The smell of coffee was the first thing she noticed.

Then the silence. Not the soft, peaceful kind she'd come to love in her own place. This was the heavy, unspoken kind that sat between people who'd run out of things to say.

Brandy opened her eyes slowly, her neck stiff from sleeping curled on the couch. Her coat was still on; her hair flattened on one side. The living room was dim, morning light barely pushing through the curtains. For a split second, she didn't know where she was.

She sat up, blinking against the dull throb behind her eyes.

And then she saw him.

Dante.

Barefoot in the kitchen, Dante stood at the stove, the deep V of his torso drawing her eyes before she could stop herself, smooth lines, and chiseled muscle. He hummed something low under his breath as he flipped pancakes, the same tune that once made her smile. Now it just reminded her of how far she'd drifted.

"Morning, sleepyhead," Dante said, turning toward her with that easy grin. The same one that used to melt her right where she stood. "You hungry? I made your favorite blueberry pancakes, extra butter."

She rubbed her forehead, trying to piece together the night. The long drive. The tense silence. The way his words had wrapped around her like a spell she knew better than to believe.

"Dante..." she started, voice barely a whisper.

He held up a hand, playful, dismissive. "Let's not start the day with all of that heavy stuff, okay? Sit. Eat. I missed this, you, me, us, mornings like this."

The way he said *us* so casually, so sure, made her stomach twist.

She sank back against the couch, fingers worrying at a loose thread on her sleeve. The coffee on the table steamed beside her, a creamy hazelnut latte. She hadn't even asked for it, but he still remembered how she took it. That was the problem. Dante remembered all the small things. And he used them like bandages to cover the wounds he caused.

Her mind replayed the night before, Sullivan's face when she walked out, the disbelief, the quiet hurt in his eyes.

The gentleness of his hand against hers in the kitchen.

The taste of sweet potato pie and the soft warmth of his lips and something that felt dangerously close to hope.

She exhaled shakily. "Dante, I don't think…"

He cut her off, sliding a plate in front of her. "Don't think," he said softly. "Just… be here. We've both been through a lot. Maybe this is God giving us another chance."

She looked up at him then. Really looked.

The bronze hue of his skin she used to memorize by touch. The precise line of his beard. Those eyes still soft, still dangerous.

He was every piece of comfort she used to crave, every reason she'd once stayed.

But now, all she saw were the cracks, the rehearsed tone, the charm that had always been more performance than sincerity.

"Everything about this," she said quietly, "feels like old wallpaper. Pretty once but peeling now."

He blinked, caught off guard. "What's that supposed to mean?"

She took a breath, steadying her voice.

"If I'm being honest," she said softly, "And if I wasn't clear last night, I came back for closure. Not love."

For a moment, he said nothing. His jaw tightened, the light in his eyes dimming to something sharp. "So that's really it, huh? You hang out with your little fake-ass friend-boyfriend for one weekend and suddenly you think you're better than me?"

Her chest flinched.

"That's not fair. And please don't gaslight me." She shifted upright on the couch, not out of fear, but sheer exhaustion from fighting the same fight on repeat.

"Three years," she said, her voice breaking into a sharp whisper. "Three years of being engaged, waiting, believing that 'not right now' meant something. And I was fine with that, fine with crumbs, until you humiliated me. You called it off before Thanksgiving, not caring about how this would look to my friends and family. You embarrassed me, Dante." She stood now, pacing to the edge of the counter. "I don't even know what I was holding on to."

She pressed her lips together, grabbed her purse. "I'm not going back and forth with you again.

She slung the strap of her purse over her shoulder, voice firm now. "You were right to call off the engagement. I should've done it first. For being a fool for you too many times. Thank you for making it easy to stop."

Silence filled the room, brittle and sharp.

Dante stared at her, something flickering behind his eyes, hurt, pride, disbelief all tangled together. "You're really done, huh?"

Brandy swallowed hard, digging for her phone. She opened the Uber app and tapped Schedule Pickup. "Like I said last night, I was done when you left."

She walked toward the door, hands trembling but her spine straight.

Behind her, the spatula clattered into the sink.

And when she stepped outside, the cold air hit her face like truth.

For the first time in a long time, it didn't sting.

THE UBER RIDE HOME was quiet except for the hum of the tires on wet pavement.

Brandy watched the city slide past in blurs of gold and gray, feeling lighter and lonelier all at once.

She should've felt guilty. Maybe she did. But mostly, she felt... done.

She pressed her palm to the window, the soft, early-morning lights flickering across her fading reflection.

For the first time in years, there wasn't anyone waiting on the other side.

Just her. And maybe, that was finally enough.

Brandy let herself into her apartment, closing the door with a slowness that didn't need to be dramatic. Just... tired. The lights were still off from yesterday. She didn't turn them on. The dark felt honest.

She shrugged out of her coat and dropped her purse on the counter without bothering to hang anything up. Her body felt heavy, not from crying-she didn't have the energy for that, but from the slow drain of going back and forth with Dante all night and into the morning.

She walked to the kitchen, toeing off her boots on the way, and reached for the bottle of buttery Chardonnay. Her hands were steady, even though her chest wasn't.

Brandy leaned against the counter, the second glass loose between her fingers. The apartment was quiet. It didn't ask anything from her.

She took another sip, slower this time. Her shoulders dropped a fraction.

Her jaw eased. Her lungs remembered how to breathe all the way down.

No tears came. No replay of the argument.

Just the tiredness that settles deep and finally stops moving. The clock on the stove blinked at 9:14 a.m. She didn't care. She set the glass down and let herself stand there in the quiet kitchen, the silence stretching soft around her. It didn't feel empty.

It felt like room. Like space she hadn't had in years. She stayed there until her heartbeat found its rhythm again. She didn't know what came next. But the ending... didn't scare her anymore.

Chapter 18

The Airbnb was too quiet. Morning light slanted through the blinds, striping the floorboards, the same boards that had groaned under his pacing half the night.

His half-packed suitcase sat open by the door, shirt sleeves spilling out like they'd given up too.

Sullivan sat on the edge of the bed, staring at the cold cup of coffee on the nightstand. He took a sip anyway, bitter, sharp, something to hold onto.

He wasn't angry. Not exactly.

Just tired in a way that settled deep and stayed there, quiet, and unmoving. His phone lay face-down on the table, but he kept glancing at it anyway. Nothing.

No missed calls. No texts. Not even a meme from Ryan.

Just silence.

He leaned forward, elbows on his knees, rubbing at the back of his neck.

The whole night kept replaying; Friendsgiving laughter, Brandy's smile in the candlelight, the way she relaxed beside him like she was finally letting herself breathe again.

And then.... Dante.

That knock. That shift.

The way her face fell when she saw him.

He'd watched her leave. Watched her walk out the door with the man who once broke her heart.

He couldn't even blame her. Hell, he wasn't sure what they were yet.

But it still stung.

The embarrassment crept in slow.

Could he have misread everything? The glances and that kiss? Maybe he'd imagined it all because it felt good to imagine something good again.

He raked a hand through his hair, a quiet laugh slipping out; tired and humorless.

"And this," he muttered, "is why I stay single."

No attachments.

No drama.

Just work, miles, and pages.

He could do pages. Pages made sense. People didn't.

His gaze drifted to the open notebook on the desk, half a paragraph of his latest draft. A love story, of course.

He exhaled through his nose, shaking his head. "Writing about brave people in love like I know what that feels like."

He thumbed through his contacts and called Rick, his assistant.

"Yo, Rick. Yeah, it's me. Listen, book me the early flight; the one out tomorrow morning. I'll meet the team a few days ahead of schedule."

Rick asked something about deadlines, burnout, the usual.

Sullivan smirked faintly. "Nah, man. Just need a change of scenery. A vacation without emotions, you feel me?"

When he hung up, the joke didn't even sound funny.

He sat back, staring out the window at the quiet street.

A dog barked somewhere in the distance.

A wind chime clinked.

Life, moving on without him.

He'd spent years writing about people brave enough to love anywhere, despite the timing, the mess, or the risk.

And when it was finally his turn, he'd folded.

He pinched the bridge of his nose, letting out a long breath. "You're a damn coward, Harper."

The soft ping of his phone broke the silence.

A message from Ryan.

Ryan: *Meet me for coffee. Can't say no either.*

He stared at it for a long moment before typing back:

Sullivan: *You always this bossy?*

The dots danced, then

Ryan: *Only when my friends need me.*

He stared at the message, lips curving despite himself.

Maybe she was right. He did need saving, from himself most of all.

MAPLE & MAIN WAS ITS usual mix of chatter and pumpkin spice, sunlight spilling through the front windows. The bell over the door chimed as Sullivan stepped inside, cold air still clinging to his coat.

Ryan waved him over from the corner table, already nursing a latte. She looked like a walking snow angel, white pea coat, fuzzy hat tipped slightly to the side, matching snow boots resting neatly under her chair.

"Hey, stranger." Her voice lifted just a little. "I ordered your usual."

Sullivan nodded, pulling off his black beanie and taking the seat across from her. His North Face jacket rustled as he settled in, the smell of roasted espresso wrapping around them. He looked comfortable but worn, black Nike shirt and joggers, a man who hadn't really slept but wouldn't admit it.

"I wanted to check on you," Ryan said softly. "I know last night got... chaotic."

He smiled faintly, though it didn't reach his eyes. "Chaotic is one word for it."

Ryan frowned, stirring her latte. "I'm sorry, Van. I didn't know Dante was going to show up. None of us did."

He shrugged, stirring his own coffee. "Wasn't your fault."

"You know I wouldn't have pushed had I thought there was any chance those two would rekindle anything," Ryan said, her tone cautious.

Sullivan's jaw flexed. "Right."

"But you liked her, didn't you?" she pressed, leaning forward, eyes narrowing playfully. "I've known you too long to miss that look."

The spoon clinked softly against his cup.

"Yeah," he admitted after a beat. "I started to like her more than I meant to."

Ryan smiled, small but knowing. "You two looked good together. Like, really good together."

He huffed out a laugh, low and rough. "Guess looks don't count for much."

"Don't do that," she said gently. "You know Brandy, she'll push people away before she admits she's scared."

He leaned back in his chair, arms crossing. "She made her choice."

Ryan's eyes softened. "Maybe. Or maybe she froze. Sometimes the right thing scares the hell out of us first."

He didn't answer. Just stared down at the table, tracing a ring of condensation with his thumb. "Yeah, well, she didn't seem scared to leave."

Ryan sighed, then reached into her bag and pulled out a hardcover copy of *If This Love Were Mine*.

He blinked, then groaned. "You've got to be kidding me."

"What?" She laughed. "I'm your biggest fan. Can I not get a personally signed copy?"

He rolled his eyes but cracked a smile. "You're ridiculous."

"Aht, aht," she teased, sliding it toward him. "Make it heartfelt. I need proof for my followers that we're actually friends."

He shook his head but pulled out a pen, flipping open the cover.

"Just drop it off at the house tomorrow," she added lightly, reaching for her cup. Then, a little too casually: "Brandy's coming over to help me get out Christmas decorations. You know me, I can't wait until December."

He looked up. "Already?"

"Already," she said, her grin widening. "If you were planning to say goodbye before you fly out, that'd be a good time."

He didn't respond right away. Just stared at the steam curling from his coffee, then at the sunlight catching the window glass.

"She'd be bummed if you left without saying something," Ryan added quietly.

Sullivan glanced outside, a couple strolled past, laughing, their gloved hands intertwined. Something about the simple ease of it ached a little.

He smiled faintly. "You always did love a setup."

Ryan grinned. "Only the good kind."

When she left, Sullivan stayed behind, staring at the half-empty cup in front of him. The shop buzzed with life around him, but his mind was somewhere else, still standing in the doorway last night, watching Brandy walk away.

He'd told himself this was easier. Leaving always was.

Until her.

As he stood, sliding his beanie back on and tucking his phone into his pocket, a thought settled heavy and clear:

He'd spent years writing stories about people brave enough to risk it all for love.

It was time to stop writing about them and finally become one.

Chapter 19

The apartment was too quiet. Brandy sat cross-legged on the couch, journal open in her lap, pen hovering above the page. She'd been staring at the same blank line for ten minutes, or longer. Every time she tried to write, her thoughts drifted somewhere else; somewhere warm. Somewhere that smelled faintly like cedarwood and warm spice.

Sullivan.

She blew out a breath, leaning back into the cushions. "Girl, get it together," she muttered, closing the journal. The page stayed empty, but her mind wasn't.

The morning after Friendsgiving bled into the next day like fog that refused to lift.

Brandy moved through her apartment on autopilot: tidying, wiping, folding, anything to keep from thinking too long. The whirr of the washing machine filled the silence. The scent of lemon cleaner clung to the air.

She'd made peace with Dante.

But peace wasn't joy.

It was quiet. Heavy, reminding her of everything she'd once carried for someone else.

For years, she'd mistaken his approval for love. The way he'd look at her when she said the right thing, or how he'd soften when she apologized first. She used to think that meant things were okay again; that she was okay again.

Now, even the thought of needing his reassurance made her stomach turn.

"This is what peace feels like," she whispered to herself, setting another folded towel on the stack. "Not begging to be understood."

Her reflection caught in the microwave door, tired eyes, messy bun, an old Duke sweatshirt she'd stolen from him years ago. She stared at it, then peeled it off and tossed it into the donation pile.

For the first time in a long time, the air around her didn't feel so small.

She went to the kitchen, poured herself a cup of coffee, and stood by the window watching sunlight break through the gray. The ache was still there but softer now. Manageable.

She missed joy.

But she didn't miss him.

That realization hit her quiet and deep, like something sacred settling in place.

Her phone rang on the counter. Desiree's name flashed across the screen.

Brandy sighed, smiling faintly before answering.

"Girl, I was just about to call you."

"Mmhmm. Don't 'girl' me. You good?" Desiree's voice was already laced with attitude and care.

"I'm fine. Just... decompressing."

"Good. Cause I was about to come over there with a bottle of Moscato and that Chunky Monkey ice cream you like and throw darts at Dante's picture."

Brandy laughed softly. "Girl you are crazy."

"Please. You know I'd do it. Listen, I love you, but you gotta stop running from what's good for you. You've been in survival mode for too long. I know it's hard to let go of what you and Dante had. But, Van was feeling you. The whole group saw it. The way he looked at you like you were the only one in the room?" She paused a beat. "You need to let somebody love you the way you deserve to be loved."

Brandy went quiet, tracing the rim of her mug. "I know."

"This time when something real shows up don't get scared. Face it. Live your life."

Brandy's eyes burned, but she refused to let the tears fall. "I don't get scared. I'm... cautious."

"Cautious, my ass. You're terrified. And it's okay, sis. Just don't let that fear talk louder than your heart."

Desiree's voice gentled. "You think he's already gone, huh?"

Brandy's chest tightened. "Yeah," she said softly. "He probably is."

The line went quiet for a moment.

"Well don't be afraid to make the first move if that's what you want. Babe, you deserve to be happy and have all the things you truly want in a man." Desiree said, before hanging up.

Brandy stood there, the echo of her friend's words floating in the still air.

She wasn't ready to chase anything. Not yet. But maybe she didn't have to. Maybe she just had to stop running.

She stood, glancing at her reflection in the mirror on the wall. Her curls were a mess, her eyes still tired, but something about her expression looked... lighter.

"Alright," she said to herself. "Let's go help decorate a Christmas tree."

She threw on her Hampton University sweater shirt. Grabbed her coat and keys, stepping out into the crisp November air.

For the first time since Friendsgiving, the world didn't feel heavy.

It just felt open.

Chapter 20

Ryan's house smelled like cinnamon pinecones and Christmastime. The front lawn twinkled with early Christmas lights, half the boxes from the garage stacked high by the door. Brandy laughed the second she stepped inside.

"Girl, it's not even December."

Ryan, wearing a red plaid headband with a matching red jogger set, covered in glitter, grinned. "And yet it's Christmas in my heart."

Brandy rolled her eyes, setting her tote on the couch. "You're impossible."

"Festive," Ryan corrected. "Now come on, help me untangle these lights before I lose my salvation."

The two of them worked in companionable chaos.

Ryan was knee-deep in a plastic bin full of tangled lights, muttering under her breath like the wires personally offended her. Brandy perched on the arm of the couch, untangling ornaments wrapped in tissue, the radio crooning old-school holiday R&B.

Glitter dusted everything: the rug, their hands, even the curls at the edge of Brandy's hair.

"Girl," Ryan huffed, holding up a half-dead string of lights, "I swear these things conspire against me every year."

Brandy laughed. "You say that like you didn't buy six new sets last Black Friday."

"That's not the point," Ryan shot back.

"These are the good lights. The ones with the soft glow, not that bright blue hospital lighting mess."

Brandy smirked, shaking her head as she unwrapped a tiny ornament shaped like a gingerbread man. "You and your 'soft glow.'

You need an intervention. I bet you already have another cart full of decorations saved online."

Ryan didn't even pretend to deny it. "I mean... HomeGoods had a sale, and I might've added a few things. You can never have too many throw pillows."

Brandy gave her a side-eye. "Define 'few.'"

Ryan grinned. "Let's just say the delivery truck knows my address by heart."

They both broke into laughter that felt good in Brandy's chest. It was nice, this normalcy; the music, the scent of cinnamon candles, the faint jingle of bells from the box she'd just opened.

For a while, it was easy to forget everything else. Easy to just be.

But whenever the laughter faded, her thoughts drifted, slipping through the cracks like cold air under a door.

The way Sullivan had looked at her before she left.

The quiet hurt in his eyes.

The softness she'd seen there and hadn't known what to do with it.

Ryan looked up from the bin, catching her zoning out. "You good?"

Brandy blinked, forcing a small smile. "Yeah. Just thinking about how fast the holidays came around."

Ryan's gaze lingered for a moment, but she didn't press. She just reached for another ornament, humming along to the music.

Outside, snow had started to fall in slow, lazy flakes.

Inside, the lights flickered to life, soft, golden, and steady.

Brandy let out a breath, something soft settled inside her. She wasn't sure if it was the season, the song playing low in the background, or the ghost of a feeling she still hadn't shaken. Ryan popped open another storage box and cleared her throat casually. "Sooo, I might have forgotten to mention something."

Brandy paused. "That tone never means good news."

"Relax," Ryan said quickly. "I may or may not have told Sullivan we were decorating today."

Brandy blinked. "Ryan!"

Brandy froze where she stood, heart thrumming loud enough to drown out the radio.

She told herself not to read into it.

Maybe he wasn't fazed.

Maybe he just wanted closure.

Maybe she could hide behind the tree skirt and fake busyness until he left.

Before she could finish, a knock sounded at the door.

Ryan winced. "May."

"Ryan!" Brandy hissed.

"I'm just saying goodbye. He's flying out tomorrow.," she sang, already halfway to the door.

Brandy's pulse climbed.

Then the door opened.

Sullivan filled the doorway, and for a heartbeat, the world just... stilled.

Six feet of quiet confidence framed by the soft glow of string lights. Camel-colored coat draped open over a forest-green hoodie. A gold chain glinted at his throat, catching the light every time he moved. His skin looked impossibly smooth, rich like melted cocoa, and his cologne, cedarwood and warm spice, hit her before he even stepped inside.

His smile was easy, unhurried, curling at the corners in a way that unraveled every bit of resolve she thought she had left. And all of Brandy's maybes scattered like ornaments rolling off the table.

For a second, neither of them said anything. The radio played softly in the background, and a single snowflake drifted past the window behind him.

"Hey," he said softly, his voice low and smooth enough to melt the chill in the air.

Brandy blinked, her throat suddenly dry. "Hey."

Ryan clapped her hands together, breaking the spell. "Well, look at that! Y'all can talk while I go get more lights from the garage." She vanished before either of them could stop her.

Sullivan stepped inside, closing the door gently behind him. The scent of his cologne wrapped around her, steady and familiar.

He shoved his hands into his pockets, that smile flickering just a little shy. "Didn't mean to interrupt the decorating party."

Brandy shook her head, still trying to find her voice. "You're fine. Ryan's... Ryan."

"Yeah," he said with a soft laugh. "She told me."

Their eyes met again, and this time, it didn't feel polite. It felt like gravity: inevitable, pulling her right back into the space she'd been trying so hard to avoid.

"Let me take your coat. Might as well get comfortable. Ryan's gonna need help stringing up those lights."

Brandy reached for his sleeve before she could stop herself. Her fingers brushed the soft fabric of his camel coat, and suddenly the air between them felt charged warm, alive. He hesitated for a heartbeat, then let her slide it off his shoulders. The weight of it lingered in her hands longer than it should have.

He looked at her then, really looked. And that look was enough to make her pulse stumble.

He asked, voice low.

"Yeah," she said, clearing her throat. "Probably safer there before Ryan ropes us into climbing something."

He chuckled, following her down the short hall.

Brandy's mind spun faster than her feet could move. She wanted to say it before it sat too heavy on her chest. "Sullivan, I just...." She stopped, words tripping over each other. "About that night. Dante showing up like that. I'm so sorry. I was... embarrassed. And honestly, done. Him and me, we're over. And he understands that now."

He paused by the counter, the morning light catching the faint gold of his chain. There, in the center of the counter, sat a single slice of sweet potato pie crowned with a dollop of whipped cream.

Brandy blinked. "What the..."

Sullivan huffed a soft laugh. "Ryan."

"Of course." Brandy folded her arms, trying to ignore how perfect the pie looked. "She's relentless."

"Persistent," he corrected, leaning against the counter, arms crossing over his chest. His stance was relaxed, but his eyes; those deep, patient eyes, never left hers.

"Look," he said quietly, "I respect that you needed to close that chapter with Dante. And if, for whatever reason, you decided to give him another shot...."

"Oh, no." She shook her head quickly, stepping closer. "We're done. I have to put me first. And with him... I wasn't."

Sullivan's expression eased, something gentle sparking behind his gaze. "And with me?"

Brandy's lips parted on a breath. "With you, it felt easy. Safe. Like maybe I could start over." The silence that followed wasn't awkward; it pulsed between them, quiet and steady, like the moment before a heartbeat.

Then Brandy arched a brow. "Sooo, Sweet Potato or Pumpkin Pie?"

He smiled slow, teasing, that grin that undid her. "What do you think?"

"Definitely Sweet Potato" She laughed. Amused at the full circle moment.

"Bingo" he said, chuckling. "But I figured maybe it's our thing now." He winked.

Brandy laughed under her breath, shaking her head. "Our thing, huh? Can't believe you remembered that."

"I remember everything about that night," he said quietly. "Even the part where I told you I wanted the first bite."

Her heart stuttered. "You're still on that?"

"Absolutely," he said, stepping closer, voice low and steady. "Let's run it back. You owe me."

The distance between them vanished, replaced by the quiet pull of something inevitable. Her hand trembled slightly as she picked up the fork, cut a small piece, and turned toward him.

He was already watching her.

The air shifted. Soft, heavy with the scent of brown sugar and cinnamon.

She lifted the fork, the silver glint catching in the light. For a moment, neither of them breathed. Then she raised it, slow and deliberate.

He leaned in, lips parting slightly, eyes locked on hers. The fork brushed his bottom lip, and time seemed to fold in on itself. He took the bite, his gaze steady, a slow smile curving at the corner of his mouth.

"Still the best pie I've ever had," he murmured.

Brandy's laugh came out as a shaky breath. Before she could speak, she leaned in. Softly at first, then with all the ache she'd been holding back.

His hand slid to her jaw, light and reverent, thumb tracing her cheek.

"You sure?" he whispered.

Brandy nodded, her voice barely a breath. "I'm sure."

The second kiss was slower, deeper. It unfolded like the memory of something they were always meant to find. He tasted faintly of brown sugar and nutmeg, and for that one suspended heartbeat, the world felt right: no hurt, no hesitation, just this.

When they finally broke apart, Brandy smiled against his lips, breath unsteady but full. "You know... I could get used to this."

He laughed softly, brushing a curl from her face. "Good. Because I'm not going anywhere this time."

A throat cleared from the doorway.

Ryan stood there, grinning, a bag of ornament hooks dangling from her hand. "Finally!" she squealed. "Took y'all long enough!"

Brandy groaned, burying her face in Sullivan's chest as his laughter rumbled through her.

Outside, snow drifted against the window, lazy and light.

Inside, something settled. Soft, certain, and new.

Epilogue

Three weeks later Snow blanketed the mountains like powdered sugar, glittering under strings of lights that wound from the cabin porch to the tall spruce tree out front. The place sat high above Wintercrest Valley, a town that looked built for postcards, gingerbread rooftops, horse-drawn carriages, and carolers bundled in red scarves.

Inside, the air buzzed with warmth and cinnamon.

Brandy stood by the fireplace, laughing as Ryan tried and failed to hang mistletoe straight.

"Ryan, it's crooked again."

Ryan huffed. "It's festive. Crooked gives it character."

Sullivan's voice drifted from behind her, smooth and teasing. "That's what she said about the Christmas tree, too."

Brandy turned, smiling as he crossed the room in a dark green sweater, sleeves pushed up, firelight glinting off the gold chain at his neck. He slipped an arm around her waist and kissed her temple, the whole world softening around that simple gesture.

This peace had become their rhythm. They didn't rush it. They didn't force it. They simply... arrived in the same place at the same time, ready now in ways they hadn't been years ago.

"You're quiet," he murmured. "What's on your mind?"

Brandy leaned into him. "Just thinking how crazy it is that a few weeks ago, I was swearing off love... and now?" She looked up at him, cheeks warmed by the fire. "Now I can't imagine not having you in it."

He brushed his thumb along her cheek. "Guess we both found what we didn't know we were looking for."

A loud cheer erupted from the kitchen.

Desiree and Marcus were mock arguing about who made the better eggnog, their voices rising over the Christmas playlist.

Jackson and Gabby were still in town somewhere, bundled in matching scarves, determined to find what the locals called the world's biggest gingerbread house. The group had made a pact after Friendsgiving to spend Christmas together, and Sullivan, ever the grand gesture guy, had rented the biggest cabin he could find overlooking the Smokies.

He just hadn't planned on the storm.

Snow fell in soft, dramatic flakes, like Wintercrest had hired a snow machine just to show off. Inside the cabin, Fabian was singing "This Christmas" off-key with a level of confidence that should've been illegal.

The front door swung open hard enough to rattle the wreath. Rick Franklin stomped inside like winter had personally challenged him to a fight. Snow covered his coat, his jaw was locked tight, and his whole expression screamed "I'm over it" in ten different languages.

"Fantastic," Rick announced, dropping his carry-on with a thud. "Flights are canceled. Roads are closed. Congratulations, everyone. We're stuck in Christmas town."

Rick, Sullivan's assistant who had flown in to help coordinate Sullivan's Wintercrest book signing later in the week, stood there with his phone in hand, equal parts annoyed and defeated.

Sullivan tried not to laugh. "Guess you're officially part of the festivities."

Rick groaned. "That's super dope, Van. Nothing says holiday spirit like watching couples make out under mistletoe."

Before Sullivan could reply, another voice floated from the couch.

"Oh, don't worry," Asha said without looking up from her laptop. "I'm sure you'll find something to complain about for the next seventy-two hours."

Rick shot her a look. "And you are?"

"Asha Stewart," she said sweetly. *"Brand strategist. Content producer. Professional vibe checker. Ryan flew me in to film all this holiday magic for her sponsor collab. You're welcome."*

Rick muttered, *"Didn't say thank you, but okay."*

Ryan appeared beside them, practically glowing.

"Oh, this is going to be fun."

Sullivan caught Brandy's eye, his grin knowing. *"You see it too, right?"*

Brandy laughed softly. *"Oh, I see it. They're either going to kill each other... or fall in love."*

He laced his fingers with hers. *"Christmas miracle, either way."*

Outside, the snow fell thicker, wrapping the cabin in white.

Inside, laughter and light filled every corner.

And for Brandy and Sullivan, this wasn't an ending. Just the next chapter.

Coming Next: Pecan Pie for Two

A Christmas Romance
Forced proximity. Holiday chaos.
Unexpected sparks between two people who swear they can't stand
each other.

Pecan Pie for Two Teaser

Chapter One

Snow drifted past the cabin windows in slow, dramatic flakes, the kind that made Wintercrest look like someone shook a snow globe until it begged for mercy.

Rick Franklin stood near the entryway, brushing snow from his coat with the energy of a man who was one minor inconvenience away from losing it. He had been stuck in this Christmas postcard for exactly thirty minutes, and he already hated every second. Couples everywhere. Lights everywhere. Mistletoe everywhere. And now? He was stranded until Christmas morning.

Fantastic.

"Seventy-two hours of this?" Rick muttered, dropping his carry-on with a thud that rattled the wreath on the door.

Ryan drifted past him with garland wrapped around both wrists like she was leading a holiday parade. She beamed. "Oh, this is going to be good."

Of course she was happy. Chaos was her love language.

Behind her, on the couch, Asha Stewart snapped her laptop shut with the satisfaction of someone ready to cause trouble on purpose.

"Try not to trip over your own attitude, Franklin," she called, lifting her camera.

Click.

Rick blinked. "It's actually Rick. And... did you just take a picture of me?"

"No," Asha said, checking her screen. "I took art."

"Well, I'm not in the mood for a documentary crew."

"Well," she said sweetly, "lucky for you, I'm not a crew. I'm talent."

From the kitchen, Sullivan laughed under his breath.

Asha stood and smoothed her Christmas sweater, fully prepared to boss the entire cabin around. Rick watched her the way someone watched a firework in a crowded room: impressed, annoyed, and ready to duck.

She lifted her camera, squinted at the fireplace, and snapped another shot. The string lights she'd arranged earlier glowed above a mug she had positioned for maximum cozy effect.

"Ryan!" Asha called. "I need a pinecone. Or a sprig. A sprig would be iconic."

Ryan shouted back from the tree. "I am busy creating winter wonderland magic. Do I look like a sprig dealer to you?"

"You look like the plug for all things festive," Asha said, adjusting her focus. "Please. I'm trying to create holiday brilliance."

Sullivan walked in wearing a cream sweater, sleeves pushed up, gold chain glinting in the firelight. He smelled like warm cologne and Christmas boyfriend energy.

"Rick, since you're staying longer," Sullivan said, "why don't you grab what they need? There's a box of seasonal nonsense in the mudroom. Top shelf. Left side. Two bags labeled 'fall stuff.' Please do not ask."

Asha nodded approvingly. "See? That is leadership. Delegation. Specificity."

Rick pressed his lips together, swallowed the words he wanted to say, and headed toward the mudroom.

He made it two steps before Sullivan clapped him on the shoulder.

"Glad you're still here," Sullivan said with a grin. "Now you can help make sure the signing runs smooth tomorrow. And Asha is filming the whole thing."

Rick stopped cold.

"She is filming... what now?"

Asha beamed like this was her favorite part of the day. "I pitched Sull a full holiday content strategy. Behind-the-scenes shots. Cozy fan moments. Branded vibes. Aesthetic pie close-ups. All extremely marketable."

Rick stared at Sullivan, betrayed. "Sull? So, we are calling you Sull now?" He laughed and shook his head in disbelief.

"You let this lady with a camera curate your book signing?" He muttered to himself all the way to the mudroom. He was supposed to be on a plane. In first class. Headed to Tulum, Mexico. Sun. Margaritas. Beautiful women.

Now? He was trapped in a snowstorm with mistletoe, matching couples, and Asha Stewart. She was exactly his type of nightmare. The kind that talked too much. Filmed too much. Knew too much. And unfortunately... the kind he wasn't getting away from anytime soon.

Thank You for Reading Sweet Potato Kisses

Thank you for spending time with Brandy, Sullivan, and the whole Pine Hill crew.

I hope their story brought you warmth, joy, and a little holiday magic.

If you loved this book, it would mean the world to me if you left a review via Goodreads or Amazon.

Your reviews help readers find the story and they help indie authors like me more than you know.

https://www.goodreads.com/book/show/243515143-sweet-potato-kisses

Thank you again, see you in Wintercrest.

With love, Nina Stewart

About the Author

Nina Stewart is a native of Chicago, Illinois, who also proudly considers Minneapolis, Minnesota her home. She is a mother of three, an Army service member, and a lifelong storyteller. Nina wrote her first books at the age of eight "Get Well Soon, Grandma" and "Me and My Little Sister Bo Bo." Even then, she knew stories were her way of loving the world.

Nina writes clean, no-spice romance because she wanted love stories that celebrate chemistry, connection, and the soft, slow beginning of falling in love without explicit scenes. Her books capture warmth, friendship, and the magic of Black love, often wrapped in cozy, holiday vibes.

When she's not writing, Nina enjoys baking, crafting, and watching every Hallmark holiday movie she can find.

YOU CAN CONNECT WITH her at:
TikTok: @authorninastewart
Instagram: @authorninastewart
Facebook: Author Nina Stewart
Website: **www.authorninastewart.com**[1]
Business inquiries: theauthorstrategist@gmail.com

---

1. http://www.authorninastewart.com

www.ingramcontent.com/pod-product-compliance
Lightning Source LLC
Chambersburg PA
CBHW050859180626
46814CB00007B/2801